(Synopsis)

Wei

As the new music professor at Korham University, I need to focus on my job. I can't get entangled with that tall and handsome Facilities Manager I keep bumping into on campus. Did we have a hot moment together at Christmas? Maybe, but that doesn't change the fact that he's taking my music lecture. Students are off limits, no matter how flirty and sexy they are.

The problem is Logan's not just a student; we're co-faculty, neighbors, and we've become good friends. I've started to peel back the layers that make up who he really is. It turns out there's more to this sweet guy whom I've been growing closer and closer to. As the semester winds down, the days of him being my student are numbered. Pretty soon, nothing will stand in the way of us hooking up. It's scary, but can an athlete like him really fall for a performing artist like me? Because I'm afraid I'm already there.

Logan

I've been broken for a long time, so I've made my job at KU my life. No one has been able to tug on my heartstrings for years. So, of course, I'm blindsided by this talented and gorgeous new professor I met. He makes me

The Strings We Play

(Artists and Athletes book 3)

By CD Rachels

The Strings We Play (Artists and Athletes book 3)

Cover Illustration Copyright © Story Styling Cover Designs

Professional beta read by Catherine at Les Court Services. www.lescourtauthorservices.com

Copy Editing by Karen Meeus. www.karenmeeusediting.com

smile and gives me something to look forward to for the first time in so long. There's only one catch: I'm taking his intro to music class.

That's fine by me; I can push down these feelings. I can totally ignore the blazing hot chemistry Wei and I have in the tiny practice rooms where he teaches me scales. But as the semester goes on, I realize he can offer me so much more than just a pretty face. It's possible that everything I lost all those years ago exist in Wei. When he plays a song, or whenever it's just the two of us, it feels like magic.

I refuse to make a move on my professor, even though we're both faculty. Good things come to those who wait, right? I just have to make sure he doesn't realize I have a massive crush on him and not let him kiss me... again. And again.

["The Strings We Play" is a low-angst, male/male romance about two working adults. It involves music lessons, workout sessions, kissing under the stars, soccer-themed birthday cakes, and discovering the love that only a found family can bring. HEA guaranteed.

It is the third book in the "Artists and Athletes" series but can be read as a standalone.]

Disclaimer

Names, colleges, characters, businesses, places, events, and incidents in this work are used in a fictitious manner. Any resemblance to actual persons, living or dead, or actual places or events is purely coincidental.

Note

To J. Thanks for letting me put a ring on it and walk down the aisle with you.

1: Wei

I'm sitting in a chair trying to get my fingers to not tap 'Für Elise' into my lap. I need to keep calm and impress the two people in front of me. I'm at the final interview for my dream job. I've always wanted to be a professor of music, and now I've made it to the Dean's office at nearby Korham University. All the pieces of my—at times crummy—life may finally be falling into place

"Your résumé is very impressive Mr. Wong," Dean Layborne says, sitting across from me at his large mahogany desk. Seated next to him is the Music Performance Department Chair, and hopefully, my new boss, Professor Reyes.

"Thank you. And please, call me Wei."

"I was thoroughly impressed with all the performance pieces you sent me," Professor Reyes remarks. She leafs through my résumé and I hope I'm not sweating. A lot is on the line here. "But I didn't realize you were so active with other organizations. It says here you were the vice president of your community college's Queer Pride Union?"

I hope this isn't a deal breaker, but I'd rather not be completely closeted at this new job. "Yes, I was. Is that a problem?"

"Not at all," Dean Layborne replies. He looks up at me and smiles, and a wave of relief washes over me. "We here at Korham are extremely inclusive. Our students represent a wide range of ethnicities, genders, and orientations. Some of them even play on our many sports teams."

I smile and nod as he keeps going. "This culture is thanks in no small part to our very own QPU. We could use another faculty advisor for that group. If you were to take this position, would that be something you'd be interested in?"

"Absolutely. I'm quite passionate about supporting the queer community and allies, alike." I try to give my most charming grin. Frankly, I'd volunteer to shovel horse manure if they asked me—anything to convince them to give me this job.

"Glad to hear it," Professor Reyes says. "Well, I think you are exactly what we're looking for in an Assistant Professor in the Music Department. Dean Layborne, wouldn't you agree?"

"Hey, I can barely play a scale, so I can't speak for performances. But you seem to be hard-working and the proper fit for our University. So Dominica, if he's good with you, he's good with me." He turns to Professor Reyes and grins. Did they both say what I think they said?

They stand up and, instinctively, I get up as well. "Well it's settled then. We'd like to offer you a faculty position for next semester." My heart starts to pound in excitement over her words. "Welcome to Korham University,

Wei."

{

My hands are shaking the entire time I fill out the paperwork at the human resources office, but I can't help it; my dream just came true. I'm going to be joining KU in January as a full-time professor. Well, my official title will be Assistant Professor because I need to keep studying music here to get my doctorate, but still! I've wanted a teaching position for so long, and it was a bit of a long shot for me. My whole life I've just been the poor Chinese kid with no parents, but now, I'm on track to becoming a full-fledged music professor. It's finally happening for me!

Before I leave the building, Professor Reyes catches up to me. "Wei, I want to talk to you for a bit."

"Sure, what's up?" *Play it cool, Wei. This is your future boss.*

"I read in your résumé that you do freelance piano gigs sometimes?"

"Yes."

"Well, there's this Athletics Formal coming up."

"The one next Saturday? I'm actually going to be here on campus."

"Really?"

"Yes. One of my other jobs is at a catering company and we'll be serving for the formal."

"Oh, how convenient! Is it at all possible for you to play piano with us? Our rhythm section is missing a decent keyboard player. It would only be for about an hour or so."

She sounds desperate, and I don't want to get off on the wrong foot with my new boss. How can I say no?

"OK, I'm sure I can slip away for an hour."

"Oh, perfect! Of course, you'll be compensated." For a brief moment I almost refuse her offer, but then I remember how many bills we have to pay at home. Some months, the freelance piano gigs are my biggest source of income.

"Sounds good. I'll see you then."

"Great. Even if you couldn't make this gig, Wei, I really believe you're going to make a great addition to the Korham University faculty."

I beam and nod at her, then walk away. I sure hope so.

The next Saturday afternoon, my sister is kind enough to drop me off at the KU Athletics Center. I'm dressed in my suit and tie, and my black hair is expertly styled in spikes in all the right places. I'm super early, but I want to get in some practice time at the stage setup since every keyboard feels different.

As I wander into the large complex, I notice lots of Christmas decorations, but no staff. The rest of the catering company won't be here for another hour. I walk past one corridor, unaware of how to get into the events space where I presume the formal will take place. Eventually, I come upon one open door to a room where I hope to find at least one staff member.

Peering in, I spot something that takes my breath away: a tall man with brown hair is putting on a white button-down shirt over his naked torso. I swear, time slows down as he shucks it on, unaware I'm standing there. I don't want to ogle, but his body is magnificent. He's got tufts of chest hair —a genetic trait I never got—and miles of muscle coursing over his six-feet=something stature.

My mouth goes dry, but I finally shake my head in an effort to speak. "Um...excuse me?" He turns to look at me, finally buttoning up his shirt. He looks to be about my age, and his brown eyes and chiseled jaw are all gorgeous. *Clearly, my gay ass needs to get laid.* "I'm looking for the music department?"

The tall guy stares at me, hands frozen, allowing me a glimpse of his perfect chest for a few moments more. He opens his mouth, but no noise comes out. Weird.

"Wei!" I turn to see Professor Reyes down the hall from this guy's office. She's standing in front of an elevator and waving me down. I turn back to the hot guy still giving me deer-in-the-headlights eyes and nod at him.

"Never mind. I got it," I mutter, turning away from his handsome face. I don't know who he is, but he just became a potential work-related perk here at KU.

2: Logan

I finish up some work in my office and put my suit jacket on. I can hear some of the student athletes starting to arrive, so I need to make my grand appearance. Locking my door, I square my shoulders and take a deep breath. "Put on a smile, Logan," I mutter to myself. Everyone is expecting the happy, cheerful version of me, not the broken one.

"Logan!" I turn to see who's hollering and spot a hoard of undergrads walking my way. It's the men's soccer team, all dressed in their fanciest clothes. As Facilities Manager of the KU Athletics Center, I have a good rapport with all the student athletes.

"You're lookin' fancy, my man!" Landee Landon, a junior, is leading the way. He's got on a black suit and his blond hair is expertly styled. Beside him are the team co-captains Ravi Metta and Kareem Hall, both also dressed appropriately for tonight's Athletics Formal.

"Who invited you punks here?" I grin at them and they all chuckle.

"Ahh, Logan, we know we're your favorites."

Omar Odom pops out from behind Landon. He's another soccer boy who rounds out their quartet of friends.

"Hey, let's all take a picture together!" Landon whips out his phone and I have no choice but to take a selfie with these boys. Smiling into the frame, I think back on my undergrad days. Is it really only six years ago that I was a carefree student athlete like them? I don't usually feel my twenty-seven years of age, but then again, I rarely take pictures with students.

After we're done taking a photo, two girls in dresses walk up to us. I presume they're the boys' dates. Next to the girls walks a skinnier guy in a suit with well-styled brown hair. He seems nervous and out of place; I make it a point to know all the student athletes, and he is not one of them.

Ravi puts his arm around the guy and the pieces start to fit together. I had heard rumors that Ravi, the big man on campus, came out as gay to his whole team last week.

"This is Logan Micucci." Ravi looks at his date, then points at me. "He runs this building. Logan, meet Steven." I smile and shake hands with Ravi's date. "He's... my boyfriend." Ravi grins at Steven, and his boyfriend looks like he's falling in love with him all over again.

"Ahh. Well you two have a good time tonight." I beam at them and hope they know I accept all orientations. How can I not? I don't do sexuality labels, but if I had to pick one, I'd identify as bisexual. "And you treat him right."

"I, uh, promise I will," Steven stammers. His face looks a bit redder.

"I was talking to Ravi." The three of us laugh, and just like that, any tension is gone.

* * *

Thirty minutes later, the Athletics Formal is well underway, and I'm standing off to the side eating some hors d'oeuvres. Work-related functions feel awkward and stifling, so I wish I could drink, but this event is to celebrate the students and their accomplishments. There's no champagne, even though I know all the college kids are going to party after and get drunk. It reminds me of a time when I used to party and have fun, before I lost it all...

"Logan, my man!" Turning to my right, I see Daniel Dacks, coach of the men's soccer team, with his wife. "You're looking sharp."

"Coach Dacks. Mrs. Dacks." I nod at them both. "You both look good as well. It's always nice to see us out of our coaching gear."

"I hear ya. Bet you didn't recognize me without a whistle on my neck."

"Exactly." I chuckle.

"So, I have some plans for next semester's practices. I was thinking we could..." His words trail off in my mind, and I swear I want to listen to him, but I just can't. To my left, the music department begins to play. At the piano is none other than the hot Asian guy who saw me shirtless earlier. Coach Dacks's voice is all but lost on me as I listen intently to the musicians.

Don't get me wrong; I don't believe in love at first sight or destiny or any of that. But as I watch him play the piano with such ease, creating magnificent melodies, I can't help but start to believe in...something new. Most days I feel numb, but seeing him on stage and hearing his music has me infatuated.

What is it about him that pulls me in, like a

sailor by a siren's song? Maybe it's the fact that he was ogling me in my office while I was getting dressed. I wasn't creeped out; keeping fit is one of the only coping mechanisms I've ever had, so I know my body is tightly built, and I don't care who sees it. I was thrilled when I caught him watching me. He was crazy handsome, and I was stunned speechless; that's a huge deal because I'm not affected by anyone nowadays.

I guess it's fortunate I spend so many late nights in my office that I keep my clothes here. Otherwise, I wouldn't have met him.

Yes, it's pathetic, but this building is my baby and my job is my life.

I nod along to whatever Dacks is saying and turn to see Ravi and Steven slow dancing. They look adorable, and I miss the days when young love was actually an option—not that I ever took relationships seriously. A moment after they start dancing, I see the hot music department guy whisper to the cellist and the drummer, then they all immediately shift to a soothing melody. Soon enough, Kareem and his date join the dance floor, prompting a slew of other student couples to slow dance.

Piano guy helped to make this magical moment happen? That is *so* sexy.

Thirty   minutes   later,   the   music

department's set is done for now, and I'm applauding like crazy. *OK, Logan, game time.* Go up to him and introduce yourself. Maybe he's gay, and maybe he'll want to be friends, but there's only one way to find out.

I make my way through the dance floor, past the crowd of dispersing students. I'm trying to be subtle and not immediately run up to my handsome target, but by the time I get to the stage, he's gone while the other musicians are still packing up.

Spinning my head around, I spot him walking toward the back where the catering staff has set up. Huh. I follow him and catch him going into the conference room where all their supplies are. Walking in, I see he's alone and hasn't noticed me yet. He's taking off his suit jacket and putting it on a chair. My pulse speeds up at seeing his lean frame tightly wrapped in a white shirt. He's shorter than me and trim, but his body looks absolutely stunning.

"We gotta stop meeting like this." He whips his head around while unbuttoning his sleeve. He looks so adorable I can't help but smile. "I see you found the music department." I attempt to give him my most flirtatious grin. It's been way too long since I've tried, but hopefully I still have *some* game.

"Uhh," he says, frozen in place.

"I saw you earlier, right? In my office?"

He shakes his head. "Oh uh, yeah. Sorry about that."

"No worries. But what are you doing back here? I thought you were part of the music department."

"It's actually a long story." He smiles and unbuttons his sleeve, and I get the urge to rip it entirely off him. "I'm here because—"

"We need those heating trays ASAP!" I turn to see one of the caterers peering her head through the doorway. "Hurry up, please, Wei. We're dying out here."

Confused, I open my mouth to speak when I hear the hot guy next to me reply, "On it. Be right there."

I turn back to him and see him putting on a red vest. He's pulled up his sleeves and looks at me sheepishly. "I should go. I'm with the catering staff."

"What? No you're not. I just saw you on stage."

He shrugs and picks up a large box filled with metal pieces. "I'm new, and I was doing the music department a favor. If you'll excuse me, I have to get back to my other job."

He's struggling to hold up the box—I can tell it's over filled—so I swoop in a grab it for him. "What are you—"

"I got it." I easily hold up the box in my arms. "Lead the way. I'll help you."

"You don't have to."

"I'm the Facilities Manager. What I say goes in this building, and I say I want to help you."

He looks like he's blushing, so I take that as a win. "OK. Thanks."

"I'm Logan, by the way," I say as we walk back to the dining area.

"I'm Wei."

"Ah, that's *way* easy to remember!" I cringe. "Sorry." *What a stupid joke.*

"It's alright. I've heard it all." He chuckles and shrugs. "Right here, please."

I place the box down, and other caterers walk up to us. Wei starts pulling out metal trays and hands them to his coworkers. The woman from before looks at me, seeming confused, but takes some trays from Wei and leaves.

"Thanks, Logan."

"Don't mention it." I smile at him.

"Well, I need to get back to work."

"Oh, OK. Well if you need any more help—"

"I got it, thanks! You should enjoy your dinner."

"Alright..." I reply, half-heartedly. For a moment, he hesitates and looks at me, before finally walking back to the line of tables with the other caterers.

Reluctantly, I walk to my seat with my hands in my pockets. I turn back to see Wei already looking at me. He snaps his eyes back down nervously, like I'm going to chastise him or something. He's so adorable.

Wei. I got a name. And he knows mine. It's thrilling. I don't remember the last time I felt this way, but I don't hate it.

3: Wei

I'm happy to say my set with Professor Reyes and the others in the music department went well. The pieces she emailed me were pretty easy and I was able to practice a little in the few days prior to coming here. I thought it was cute to see all the student athletes on the dance floor. One biracial gay couple looked so sweet that I had to stop and tell the rest of the musicians to play a slow song just for them.

Now it's the end of the night, and I'm back to being part of the catering group. Most of the students and coaches are gone, so it's our job to pack and clean up. A bunch of our staff left already, leaving me to do the cleanup, while someone brings around our van. I've mostly gotten accustomed to this job, and between this and the piano gig, I'll be able to buy decent Christmas presents this year. Once I'm working at KU for real, I'll have a steady income and eventually benefits—score!

I'm wrapping up a large tablecloth when I notice someone else is folding it up as well on the other side. Logan, the sexy Facilities Manager, is helping me pack up for some reason. I tried so hard not to stare at him in his suit all night while I was serving, but now he's standing across from me, smiling. He's removed his jacket so I can see more of how his white shirt hugs his sides, and he looks delicious.

"Hey," I greet him awkwardly.

"Hey yourself." He moves closer to me, helping me fold up the corners of the cloth. "Do we put it in this box?"

"Yeah, we wash them all later, so I just fold them and stack them." I feel my face get warmer as I shift some fabrics around. "So, do you do this often? Clean up with strangers?"

"Yeah! Well, no...sometimes. I mostly stick to the locker rooms. But this whole building is under my jurisdiction."

"This is our responsibility as caterers." I'm hurrying over to the next table to continue cleaning up. *Why am I rebuffing him? He might actually be flirting with me!*

"I want to help, though," Logan says, easily keeping up with me. "I have to make sure my building is treated right, anyway. So please, let me help you, Wei."

I know I'm blushing at the sound of my own name. "Alright."

I fold up more tablecloths and Logan continues. "So you're a caterer *and* a musician. That's awesome!"

"Yeah, well, you're a tall and fit facilities manager." I cringe at my feeble attempt to flirt. Looking up, I see a charming grin on his face.

"Yup. I guess that makes us"—he leans in close to me and places the cloth into my box—"co-faculty."

I nearly shiver at the sound of his deep voice inches away from me.

"Well..." I walk to the next table. "Not yet. I

don't start working here until next semester."

"But you were doing the music department a favor?"

"Yeah, anything to help out."

"That's so generous of you. You're so talented, I can see why they asked for you to join in."

I'm sure I'm plum red now. "Thanks."

We spend the next ten minutes folding up the last of my catering supplies and loading them onto a cart. Logan is easy to talk to, and he makes the work go by quickly. I keep staring at his arms and chest as he lifts up objects. Even in a shirt, the man is a work of art. Not to mention the marvel of his ass in those tight suit pants when he picks up a stray fork on the ground. *Heaven help me, he's so fine.*

"How long have you been playing?"

I pick up the last tablecloth. "Since I was really little. It was the only thing I could do to entertain myself at home. We couldn't afford video games or anything. Then in elementary school, my teachers discovered I was pretty good and...the rest is history!"

I fold up the tablecloth and move close to Logan and his eyes shine. "That's so cool. I suck at music. I actually signed up to take a music class here next semester."

"Oh really?" I put more things away into another box and try to avoid eye contact with him. The idea of him being around the music department with me makes me feel...intrigued.

"Yup!"

"That's great. What made you want to take it up now?"

Logan shrugs. "I've always been more of a sports guy, but I've been seeing these student athletes take the arts requirement. These are big guys, and they're taking dance and charcoal drawing and whatnot; it makes me want to be a more well-rounded person."

We're almost done, so I move all the boxes onto the metal cart we use to transport supplies during our events. "That's great. I'm a huge proponent of that. Meanwhile, I barely exercise, so I have the stature of a twig."

"I wouldn't say that." He smiles at me again, and butterflies start dancing around my stomach. "So you work here and you do piano gigs?"

"I'm a caterer too."

"That's awesome. You're a real hot commodity."

Everything he says sounds like innuendo but I'm trying to keep my cool. "Well, I need the money." I point to my vest. "Catering isn't the most lucrative job."

"True, but money isn't the most important thing. It can't buy everything," he says, wistfully. He looks to the side, and his eyes get a faraway look in them. Before I can ask, he's back to a full smile, and he presses the button for the elevator to pick me up. I smile back, but a part of me wants to know what he meant.

Seconds later, I get off the elevator, pushing the cart, and make it to the front lobby to find Logan bounding up the stairs. With his long, thick legs, I'm sure he had no problem getting up here so fast.

"Thanks for all your help." I smile at him and stop before I get to the doors.

"Again, not a problem." He walks close to me and looks like he wants to hug me goodbye. It's only us in the Athletics Center lobby, surrounded by twinkling Christmas decor, and there's an awkward tension.

I play with my fingers on my thighs and look around nervously. "Actually, I should be thanking you," Logan says. I get a good look at him and notice his deep brown eyes are shining. His stubble adds to his sexiness, but he looks to be about my age. "These formals are usually so boring and sterile. But getting to know you, it was pretty fun."

"Aw no, I'm really not that fun." I wipe my face to cover how smitten I am with him. I don't remember the last time I flirted with someone or the last time someone was attracted to me.

"No, you are, Wei! You're easy to talk to. Plus, you're so talented. I loved listening to you play. I hope I can..." He steps forward and reaches for my hand but pulls back before he makes contact. My heart is beating out of my chest. "Maybe I'll see you around campus in the new year."

"Yeah, definitely," I reply, my voice hoarse. "Have a good holiday. I'll...see you." I turn around and take my cart and push it out the glass door. Logan rushes forward and opens it for me. I nod at him, but as I walk through, I pause right next to him. He stands almost half a foot above me, but I stare intently into his warm eyes.

He looks up and my gaze follows to what he's spotted; right above us in the doorway a branch of mistletoe is tied to the ceiling. When I look back down, he's already looking at me, eyes flaring with desire.

Ah, screw it. I tip-toe up and kiss him softly and slowly on the cheek. His stubble pricks me, but it feels so good to be able to kiss another man that I couldn't care less. When I pull back, he looks shocked.

"It was...mistletoe." I shrug. He's still not saying anything, staring at me open-mouthed, so I turn back to my cart and push my way out the door. The cold winter air hits my face, but my cheeks are still burning up.

I push my cart toward my coworker, who is waiting with the van, and replay the events of the week in my head. Getting a position at KU, then getting to meet a handsome guy like that? Maybe my luck is changing after all.

4: Logan

Once Wei is out of sight, I pump my fist, knowing no one's around. Turns out I've still got game, or maybe it was a Christmas miracle. Either way, tonight was magical in so many ways.

It's past midnight when I finally start my car and drive home. As I cruise through the darkness, I reflect on how alive I felt tonight. Meeting Wei, seeing the hungry look in his eyes in my office, then getting to flirt with him made me feel like my old self. I felt young again, like the carefree twenty-one-year-old who had so much love to give everyone. *That* Logan was a flirtatious rebel who slept with every guy or girl he was interested in. Now I can barely do an anonymous hook-up without feeling more hollow than before. Forget about dating—trying to be happy with another human in my life sounds like a nightmare.

But tonight? Tonight I got to pretend my life was OK. I got to be a prince charming type for the first time in so long. To top it off, Wei had flirted with me and kissed me! I put my hand on my cheek; I can still feel the tingling sensation where he left an invisible mark. I already thought of him as handsome, but seeing him play the piano so flawlessly was phenomenal. He was like a comet passing through the night, igniting me for the first time in over six years. I can only hope he'll crash back into my life.

Four weeks later, I'm in my office in the Athletics Center mindlessly filling out the monthly budget reports. I do a pretty good job with the sheets and allocating the funding, considering I never officially graduated from college. I was doing alright as a business major here at KU before my life got fractured and I chose to drop out.

Dean Layborne has all but begged me to take courses here at the university. As a member of the faculty, I get one free course a semester. For some reason, this year I finally relented, and, for fun, I'll be taking a beginner music performance class. I don't believe in destiny, but maybe some higher power knew I'd meet a hot new Assistant Professor who's fantastic on the piano. I'm hoping Wei can teach me a thing or two. Maybe, over time, I'll eventually get a chance to return his Christmas kiss.

But that might not ever happen. This higher power must be cruel because I've spent the past two weeks roaming the Fine Arts building's music corridors in an attempt to "accidentally" bump into Wei, but to no avail. I know that students only started moving back in for the spring semester two days ago, but I was hoping to catch him beforehand. He said he was faculty, but I don't see his office anywhere. Of course, every time I see someone in the halls, I quickly fiddle with my phone and make for the nearest exit. I don't want anyone thinking I'm a stalker or something!

Maybe that's exactly what I am, though. I'm pathetic.

A knock on my door jolts me out of my own thoughts. One of our deliverymen has arrived with the latest shipment of foam kick boards for the pool, and he needs me to sign off on the inventory. As I step out of my office and look at the massive stack of cardboard boxes, I notice a small crowd in the lobby. Between semesters, the university opened up a smoothie/coffee kiosk, and it seems to be garnering lots of attention. A line of students has gathered around it.

My heart starts to race upon seeing a familiar head of spiky black hair. I sign the delivery pad and power-walk over to behind the coffee bar. While several people are ordering and some are sitting down at the three small tables on the wall, I only have eyes for one person. Wei is by himself, drinking tea. He's wearing a brown blazer and a red bow tie—he looks so damn good.

OK, Logan, play it cool. Come up with a sexy line to get him to go out with you.

I shake my shoulders and square my frame, puffing my chest up. Game time.

"Logan Micucci!" I hear the familiar shrill voice of my colleague as she steps in front of me. Apparently she just got her coffee order and now has her sights set on small talk with yours truly.

"Professor Hark."

"So formal, we've been working together for over a year. Call me Aggie!" She flips her curly brown hair and I try to subtly side step her. I swear Wei looks up at me for the briefest moment before I'm forced to look back down at Hark.

"You are a sight for sore eyes," Hark says.

"Why is that?" I notice she has a coffee in one hand and multiple books in the other arm. I look at Wei again, who takes a sip but seems to be looking up and around, as if purposefully trying to avoid my gaze.

"Well, look at you. You're so tall and strong! Do you mind?" She moves her book-filled arm closer to me and I'm obliged to take the load off her hands. "I'm surprised you're not like a professor of biceps or something!" She cackles at her own joke while I readjust my arms to hold all of her hardcover books. "Walk with me while I finish my coffee!" Everything she says is loud and over-the-top, but she's friendly and ultimately harmless.

After she takes a long sip, we walk over to the opposite wall, far from where Wei is sitting. I keep trying to glance at him but Hark keeps staring me down, grabbing my attention. "So how was your New Year's?"

"It was fine."

"Mine was boring. No one to kiss at midnight *if ya know what I mean.*"

"I always know what you mean, Professor Hark." I put the books on the small table where she's sitting.

"I told you, it's Aggie! Come sit with me."

Reluctantly, I take a seat. I position myself so that I'm able to make eye contact with Wei. He's far, but he's alone, and I think he sees me, too.

"So, how many girls' hearts did you shatter over

winter break, Logan?"

"I don't—"

"And more importantly when is it going to be my turn?" She winks and takes a sip and I stare at her with my eyebrows furrowed.

"Um—"

"I'm just joking! A little co-faculty fun! Hahaha!" She's once again in hysterics at her own joke and Wei gives us an odd look. I hope this doesn't look like a date. *Shit.*

"Um, shouldn't you be taking these books back to the Fine Arts building?"

"Ugh, you're right." She gives another dramatic hair flip. She picks up one of the books. "I have to direct *Romeo and Juliet* this semester. How cliché, how banal. It's like the 'Jingle Bells' of theater!" She gets up to throw away her now empty cup and I see Wei is doing the same. He's headed for the exit but doesn't even glance at me. Crap, I've missed my chance. "Next semester we're doing an obscure play. Mark my words."

"Words marked," I reply, feeling defeated. Wei is gone, and he may have seen me with Hark and misinterpreted the situation.

"Well, this was fun!" She hugs me and I sit there, stiff. "Let's catch up over coffee again some time!"

"Uh, sure."

She does another hair flip then grabs her stack of books. A minute later, she's out of my lobby. I go back to my office with a renewed sense of hope. Sure, I didn't catch Wei or ask him out, but I know he definitely works at my school. Now I gotta be ready to get my flirt on the next time I see him.

I don't know what it is about him; I've only met him once, but I'm already feeling more optimistic about something than I have in years.

5: Wei

"Why are you all dressed up, Uncle Wei?"

"Because it's my first day of teaching." I'm waiting at the bus stop two blocks down. My nephew Galen is walking circles around the bus stop sign, and I shiver, keeping my hands tucked in my pockets. "So I'm going to school too."

"But you're a grown-up!" He continues to walk in circles and I'll never understand how seven-year-olds have such energy at not even eight in the morning. "You don't need to go to school!"

"Well I'm going to be a teacher there." I don't have time to explain to a first grader I'm taking classes part-time to get a PhD in Music as part of my employment at KU. Galen's hat starts to dip, so I reach over and push it on his head. "You're not cold, kiddo?"

"No. Why don't you teach at my school?"

I chuckle and notice my breath waft in front of me. "You'd like that?"

"Yeah, we could play during recess! I could

show you how to play kickball or soccer, and you'd be on my team."

"I'm not much of a sports guy; you know this, Galen." I smile at him endearingly. Despite being outside at this hour, I'm glad to be close to my nephew. He only has his mom and his uncle—my sister, Pei, and me—for family, but I'm going to make sure he's supported his whole life. We're never going to leave him when he needs us the most, unlike what happened to us. He's going to have all the things I never had, except maybe an uncle who enjoys playing sports.

"We play sometimes during gym class too!"

"Oh, look! The bus is here." I interrupt Galen before he goes on another description of his favorite games to play. Pei and I have zero athleticism, but this kid is obsessed with sports. I wouldn't be surprised if he's bound for the Olympics, go figure.

When the yellow school bus pulls up, I crouch down to Galen's height. "Now you be good during your after school program. I promise I'll pick you up after. Your mom gets home late, so we'll be making dinner for her."

"OK."

I hug him. "Love you, kiddo."

"You too, Uncle Wei. But you're squishing me." I laugh, let go, and push his hat down, nice and snug.

"You're growing up so fast; I could never." I grin as he gets on the bus. As soon as they're gone, I start the long trek down to the community bus stop. I hope they're on schedule so I can make it to KU on time.

The bus was *not* on schedule. It's my first day; I have to be present for Professor Reyes' lecture, and I'm friggin' late. Fortunately, I'm not teaching today—at least, I hope not.

I finally find the large music room and push through the double doors. Twenty students turn their heads my way. Apparently, I interrupted Professor Reyes. There's sweat on my brow, I'm out of breath, and I'm probably pale from the cold winter air. *Way to make a great first impression, Wei.*

"And that's my expectation for lecture days," Reyes says. She beckons me to the desk chair next to her while talking to the class. "You'll all be learning piano one-on-one from my Assistant Professors."

I make my way down the stairs on the left side of all the desks, trying to calm my breathing. It's my first day; I need to look presentable to these undergrads, not like the flustered new guy I currently present as. When I finally take off my bag and sit down, I tune in to Reyes's lecture.

"To my left is one, Assistant Professor Felipe. And over here, we have Assistant Professor Wei!"

I smile and wave at the class. One face in particular catches my eye while Professor Reyes continues on about the health benefits of learning an instrument. It's the same face I saw two days ago when I was getting tea at the Athletics Center. Logan looked so horrified that day, but I would be scared too if a random guy who kissed me saw me while I was out with my girlfriend.

Did I wander around the Athletics Center for hours just to pretend to accidentally bump into him again? Only a crazy stalker-type person would do that, so of course I did. I needed to know if we had a connection. Seeing him with that woman snuffed out the tiny kindling of hope I had for him. I should have known better. A guy like that—with his broad shoulders, rippling abs, and easy smile—would definitely have a girlfriend. I should not have interpreted his friendliness as flirting, and I *definitely* shouldn't have used the mistletoe magic as an excuse to kiss him.

And now it seems he's taking my class this semester. I make eye contact with him sitting in the crowd as the professor continues to talk, and his eyes sparkle with recognition. A shy smile grows on his face, and I can't help but smile back.

I can hear my shameful conscience say "Way to go, Wei. You kissed a straight guy. To make matters worse, he's one of your students. You committed a student-teacher violation before your first day. That's gotta be a record somewhere."

I look down and frown. This semester is off to a *wonderful* start.

6: Logan

He's here, he's here, he's teaching my class. Ohmygod I can't believe it.

I'm sitting in the "Basics of Music Performance 111" lecture trying not to freak out, but I can't help it. Wei is here! I knew there was a slight chance he'd be teaching the intro course I decided to take—for learning purposes, not for a degree or anything—but I didn't think destiny would be so kind!

He looks damn good too. His hair is all disheveled in a sexy way. He's got a black peacoat on over a white-and-brown plaid shirt that frames his body quite nicely. As I stare at him and try not to drool, he vacillates between smiling at me knowingly and avoiding my gaze entirely, looking uncomfortable. I don't know what that means, but now I have plenty of excuses to spend time with him.

I know that makes me sound like a horn-dog, but I actually do want to learn the fundamentals of playing piano.

* * *

Minutes later, the professor has finished up, and students are moving around as class is dismissed. I want to make a bee-line to talk to Wei, but I'm halted by an undergrad. It's Paul, a freshman soccer player.

"Mr. Micucci, I thought I saw you here."

"I already told you, it's Logan."

"Sorry." Paul winces. "I forgot."

"You're too polite for your own good, man."

"Right." He shrugs. "So what brings you to this class?"

I don't want to be rude, but I keep trying to look over Paul's shorter stature to make eye contact with Wei. Everyone's moving around, and it looks like he's conferring with the other two faculty at the front. "Well, you know...I wanted to learn music." I resign myself to looking back down at Paul. "Gotta start somewhere, might as well do it here at work. I heard we had a good music program here."

"Awesome."

"And you?"

"There's the KU arts requirement." He walks up the stairs, and I follow him. As we go, I try to subtly look back down at Wei, craning my neck. "I've always wanted to learn music theory. Besides, I heard Landon complaining about having to take a dance class as a junior."

"Oh yeah," I mumble, still only half paying attention.

"He sounded so distraught, and I didn't wanna be like Landon."

"Say no more. I've heard that many times in the past year."

We laugh at Landon's expense and walk out if the lecture hall. Before I close the door, I look back down and see Wei following Professor Reyes through a back entrance. He glances up at me, then immediately darts away.

If I didn't know any better, I'd say he's avoiding me.

Today, he can't avoid me. As part of the class, we needed to sign up for private lessons with the Assistant Professors in half-hour chunks. Naturally, I picked Wei's time slot, so we have no choice but to spend time together.

The prospect of the two of us being alone in a room together, playing music, thrills me to no end. Before I met him, no one could hold my interest, but now? I'm actually looking forward to something for the first time in years.

I make it to the underground practice room right as the previous student is leaving. The music wing of the Fine Arts building is composed of the large lecture hall we're in half the time and several practice rooms lining the corridor next to it. Each room is locked, but when I gazed into the windows of each door over winter break, I could see various instruments and music stands.

The blonde girl walks past me and out walks Wei from the open door. He looks so shocked to see me. "Oh hello, um…"

"It's Logan." I smile.

"Right. I remember," he mutters, still not looking at me. "Come on in."

I walk into the tiny room and sit on the bench. I place my required beginner sheet music on the piano stand and hear Wei close the door. *Cool your jets, Logan.* You're just confined in a tiny, private room with a hot guy. You're here to learn, not to jump his bones.

"I'm Assistant Professor Wong. But, um, as Professor Reyes, said, you can call me Wei." He's wiping his hands on his khakis and he's still not looking me in the eyes.

"Hi, Wei." I grin and he looks at me. "I'm glad to be here. Taking this class."

"Yes, well." He audibly swallows then blinks twice. "I'm glad to be, um, of service."

My smile broadens and I try not to get too aroused by his wording. "Well, I do want to learn the fundamentals of piano."

"That's good because I'm going to be grading you."

"I have you for the next twenty-four minutes or so. Here, in this room." Yeah, I'm playing the innuendo game.

"Mhm!" He squeaks.

"So teach me." I smile and take him in. His hair is perfectly spiky, like at Christmas. His cheerful face is gone, now replaced with nervousness. He looks so distraught, like, I'm going to hurt him. I wonder why…

"So then, let's start with exercise one. Now place your right thumb right there." I move my hand to where he's pointing. "That's Middle C."

By the end of the first lesson, I'm finally able to play a simple scale with both hands together—no easy feat for a first-timer! I fumbled a bit at first, but Wei was super patient as he showed me how to read music and where to put my fingers.

"Good job!" He seems so relaxed ever since we started really getting into the music. I knew this was his element ever since his performance at the formal, but apparently talking music makes his anxiety go away. I need to keep that in mind for future reference. "Keep practicing, and you'll gain finger strength and coordination. For the next lesson I'm sure you'll be ready to move on to actual songs."

"Thanks. Do you practice in these rooms?"

"Sometimes, when I have the time. I'm the faculty advisor for Queer Pride Union now, and I'm still finding my way around campus."

"Queer Pride Union, huh?" I look up and shrug. "Maybe I can stop by sometime. I'm not a student but..." I'm not sure how to end that sentence.

"Oh, um, straight allies are totally welcome as well." Wei plays with some papers at the piano for seemingly no reason. He's not looking at me anymore, and I start to feel the awkward tension return.

"Well, it wouldn't be accurate to categorize me as straight." He whips his head around in obvious surprise.

"Oh...*Oh*!" He shrugs. "Well I saw you with your girlfriend and I assumed so—"

"What girlfriend? I don't have a girlfriend."

"I saw you with that woman and—"

"First you assume I'm straight, and next you assume I have a girlfriend." I grin, teasing him. "You're doing a lot of assuming, Professor." I smile and stand up, all packed up and ready to go.

"I wasn't...I don't..." He's stammering and looking up.

"Wei, are you uncomfortable because you thought I had a girlfriend when you kissed me?"

His eyes dart left and right, and this little piano room suddenly feels a lot warmer. "I...wasn't going to bring it up." His cheeks redden and he looks so cute.

"Kind of a big elephant in this tiny room, don't you think?" I say in my flirtiest tone. His eyes finally meet mine, and I can tell there's so much he wants to say.

"Logan, I—" A knock on the door snaps us out of it.

"Hello?" I hear a younger woman's voice on the other side of the door. Fortunately, there's a paper sign over the tiny window, so she can't see us in here directly. "Professor Wei? It's my session now."

He coughs, and I open the door. "Sorry. We were running late."

"Don't forget to uh...practice those scales!" Wei says in an oddly mechanical tone.

I walk out and the student walks in after me. Before the door closes, I give Wei one last meaningful stare. I smile, and he pauses before shutting the door.

I'm already counting down the minutes until next week's private lesson.

7: Wei

I put some of the fried tofu on a plate and carry it over to our small kitchen table as I hear my sister step out of her room. I lay out the other two plates and some chopsticks while Galen toys with his chicken nuggets and plays on his tablet.

"Thanks again," Pei says, walking into the kitchen. Her hair is still damp from the shower as she pulls out the chair next to her son. "What do we say to Uncle Wei?"

"Thanks for the chicken nuggets!" Galen responds without looking up.

I giggle. "You're welcome kiddo. There's some more rice in the cooker, Sister."

"Mhm," she replies, already devouring some tofu. Working in healthcare, I know she's on her feet twelve hours a day, so I'm sure she's hungry. The two of us have gotten so used to cooking and fending for ourselves, but nowadays we try to have dinner as a three-person family regularly. Ever since Galen was two or so, Pei and I agreed we wanted him to have a stable childhood he could remember fondly.

"How was school? For both of you." Pei finally makes eye contact with me as I eat some rice. "You first, actually. How is KU?"

"It's great." It really is, but I feel like I'm hiding something. I typically tell my sister everything, but not about relationships. She's only a year older than me, and we've been a duo for as long as I can remember. My aunt, who was our legal guardian, was always emotionally aloof, but she put a roof over our heads and food on the table, so she wasn't awful. Still, it's always been us against the world. Growing up, we worked a lot and saved as much money as we could, and it came in handy when Pei got pregnant and her boyfriend ran away.

"Are you making friends?"

"Shouldn't you be asking the kiddo that?"

"I have friends, Uncle Wei!" He's smiling at me and I grin back.

"You've barely eaten your dinosaur nuggets, sweetie," Pei replies, turning to him. Galen takes a bite of one and proceeds to play around with another, like they're real dinosaurs.

"I'm serious, Brother." She's turned her focus back to me. "I know how much you were looking forward to it."

"I know. And I like it." I get up to get more rice and to evade her perceptive stare. Pretty soon she might find out I'm hiding something, the fact that I've made one very *very* good friend on campus.

"How is the commute? I know you got out pretty late yesterday."

"I had to stay for the group I'm the faculty

advisor for. My cab made it back to the bus stop in time to pick up Galen."

"Great. Have you found anyone to hang out with?"

I raise an eyebrow at her. "These kids are like, ten years younger than me, so no."

"What about co-faculty?" My mind flashes back to a pair of kind brown eyes, but there's no way I want to talk about Logan right now.

"Nope. Why do you ask?"

"I just think, with this job, it'll be nice for you to have a social life."

"I'm busy navigating the campus, teaching classes, practicing, and QPU on top of it all." I shrug.

"What's QPU?" Galen asks.

"It's um..." I look at Pei, who shrugs at me. "It's a group for grown-ups."

"QPU sounds like Pikachu!" Galen eats another nugget, and hopefully that's the end of that conversation. I'm not ready to explain to my nephew what "queer" means and how it describes me, at least not today.

"Don't talk with your mouth full, sweetie." Pei turns back to me. "I'm just saying I want you to be happy and healthy, and part of that means having friends."

I know her concern comes from a good place, so I nod. We lacked a close parental figure growing up, so my sister and I have always had each other's backs.

"Also, if the commute is bad, you can borrow the car when I'm off," Pei says.

"I can take the bus. There's only one transfer."

"Are you sure? If I'm off—"

"It's fine. You need it for errands and stuff."

My sister slowly nods like she doesn't believe me but doesn't push it. We both sit there quietly eating the rest of dinner.

Two hours later, I'm washing the dishes while my sister puts her son to bed. As I do, my thoughts drift back to Logan. What were the chances the super hot guy I met at Christmas would be my student? And he implied he's also queer? The odds must be astronomical. I don't *ever* meet men who want me. On top of that, I know he's not a minor or anything, and we're technically both faculty, but I can't help but feel morally grossed out.

Did I cross a line? Well, no, he wasn't my student when I kissed him on the cheek—his firm, warm, stubbly cheek that smelled so sexy.

My throat goes dry as I finish the last pair of chopsticks and put them on the drying rack.

I'm an Assistant Professor now. I can't go around having crushes on students. Do the athletes on campus have nice bodies? Sure, noticing them is unavoidable, but they're all like ten years younger than me. I could never have feelings for them. Logan, however, is not. He's about my age, we work together, and simply being around him gets me all hot and bothered. But alas, he's my student.

I turn off the lights and go down to the basement. Our house is small, but it's ours, and I've made my own space on the lower floor. Next to the laundry machine, there's a wall with a door that locks. I have a bed, a PC, a desk, and a chair so I can work. Most importantly, I have a music stand and an electric piano, so I can practice my craft in private.

I crawl into bed and pull up the comforter. As I drift asleep, I pray for the safety of my family. It was only the two of us for so long, a brother and sister trying to make our way in the world. Now we both have this little one whom we love more than anything, and we're going to make sure he has the normal childhood we never did.

8: Logan

I'm in the piano room again, fumbling through a two-handed rendition of 'Row, Row, Row your Boat'. I'm a bit of a nervous wreck, and it's not just because I have a crush on the handsome professor sitting right next to me. Playing music is so out of my wheelhouse, and every time I make a mistake, I wince. My misplayed notes don't seem to faze Wei, much to his credit.

"Good job."

"You don't have to lie."

"I'm not," he replies. "Lying, that is. It's good you're making progress. That's the important thing."

"I keep flubbing up my left hand." I frown and stretch my fingers.

"Don't be so hard on yourself. You're new, and you're learning. That's why you're taking this course."

"I sound like...What's the word we learned about in class? When things don't go together?."

"Dissonance."

"Yeah. When I want my music to sound like...

that question on the quiz I got wrong? When two notes are spaced the right amount of length?"

"Harmony." He outright giggles and plays three perfect notes, then plays them all at once.

"See? You're so awesome, and I'm so...meh. It sucks not being good at it."

"It's new."

"Yeah, but give me an exercise machine, and I can do bicep curls, flies, and pull-ups for days. It was always so easy for me."

I turn to see Wei already smiling. "See? That's your strength—literal strength training. I could never do that."

"Come down to the faculty gym in my center some time. I could teach you a thing or two." I have to hold back from winking, but there's plenty of innuendo in my voice.

Wei's eyes seem intrigued, but he immediately looks down. "Yes, well..." He clears his throat. "I think we're about done for today."

I stand up and put my plan into action. "Thanks, Wei. Um, what are you doing now?" I chose the final time slot online, knowing he would be done after. That way, I could ask him to hang out.

"I'm going to go practice right now."

"Really? Right here?"

"No, actually." He stands up, closes the piano, and pushes the seat in. "It's for another instrument I'm learning. I'm taking independent study classes for my doctorate here."

"Oh." I try not to sound too disappointed. "Well I don't want to distract you too much then."

"No, it's..." His voice trails off and he looks at me. He pauses, and I'm hoping he wants to kiss me again. "Actually, do you want to come with me?"

"Hm?" I have no idea what he's getting at, but if your crush asks you to go somewhere, you go with him.

Wei grins. "Follow me. It'll be our little secret."

Damn, is he going to let me give him a blow job in a closet in the Fine Arts building? I want to be an adult and say that's a bad idea, but I'm so down.

I follow Wei into another room two doors down. He takes out a key and puts it in the knob. "This is a passion project of mine." Once he opens the door, I follow him into what looks like a slightly larger practice room.

"What is all this?" Inside, there's a small desk, chair, a tiny window that opens to a brick wall, and one very large gilded harp on a stand.

"It's kind of like my office? It's really the harp room." Wei sits down on the bench near the harp. "I'm not supposed to let anyone in here because all this is expensive."

I smile. "You're letting me in your secret room?"

Wei's smile falters, and he looks down. After a moment, he grabs the harp and pulls it toward him. "You said you felt bad you sucked at your piece. Well, time to watch me... suck?"

I giggle and feel my face get warm. "What do you mean?"

"I've always wanted to play the harp." Wei shakes his hands out. "I want to do part of my doctorate in harp performance. I'm so new at it, but Professor Reyes is letting me use the school's harp. Isn't it beautiful?" he gushes and stares at the entire frame.

"It's a Ravenna 34 string floor harp with a built-in stand! No pedals, but there's enough strings, and the levers work great, so I can play in so many different octaves and keys!" He sighs and drags his hand over the top of the frame. I feel like I'm watching an advertisement, and he lost me with the description. He's so passionate. It's actually pretty sexy.

"Wow," I say, beaming. "I've never seen you like this before."

"Yeah, I'm a music nerd. What can I say?" He grins like a kid opening a birthday present.

"I think it's cool."

"Well, I'm new at this, so I'm fumbling with all the fingerings and where to put my hands." He shrugs and strums two strings. "I don't know if you want to watch me play. It proves everyone has to start somewhere, even people like me."

I smile and nod. Wei immediately looks down. "Sorry, this is probably super lame. You can go if you—"

"No!" I blurt. "It's not." I sit down and cross my arms. "I'd love to listen to you play."

"I'm going to be messing up a lot." His face looks redder as he stares at the strings.

"Hey, watching you practice will inspire me to practice. So you're doing your job."

He smiles at me, and I take that as a win. He begins to play; at first, he does some scales, but eventually gets up to short melodies. I don't say a word for the next twenty minutes.

True to his word, he messes up a lot, but listening to Wei play makes me feel something I haven't felt in over six years: relaxed.

9: Wei

After I lock up my office, Logan and I walk out of the Fine Arts building. Being with him makes me feel light, like I can handle all my responsibilities and just be chill. I get to just be a guy, not an uncle, musician, or caterer, but simply a dude with a friend. Talking to him puts me at ease, and he makes me smile. I get the urge to kiss him on more than one occasion, but I need to ignore it for many reasons.

"That was fun," he says, walking down the sidewalk. We're on a path toward the Athletics Center and one of the bus stops, which is my destination.

"Yeah, it was." I actually mean it. The sun has nearly set, and the sky casts a gorgeous purple glow on campus. Logan looks beautiful cast in the sunset, just like always. "Where you headed now?"

"My office in the center. I have some work to catch up on."

"Ah."

"You?"

"Bus stop. I'm headed home."

"Where do you live?" We walk down a cement stair case and no one's around. I feel so comfortable around him, like we've been friends for years.

"About thirty minutes down the parkway."

"North?"

"Yeah. Do you know where Dugan's Brook is?"

"Yeah," he beams. "I live near there."

"Ah." I don't know why that response thrills me.

"Maybe I can give you a ride some time." Oh, that's why.

"Oh no, no thank you." My instinct to refuse any help kicks in. "I couldn't possibly…"

"It's no problem at all. It'll be nice to have someone to talk to on my commutes."

My face gets warm despite the winter air. "I still don't want to bother you." The bus usually takes so long, and the thought of being with Logan in a tiny car is kind of a turn-on. *Why am I refusing this?*

"Well, if you change your mind, text me." We had exchanged numbers right before the lesson, for innocent, educational purposes…probably.

I stop in front of the path leading to the KU Athletics Center and turn to him. Before I can say goodbye, he asks "Hey, would you like to get lunch with me tomorrow?"

I shouldn't. He's my student. I bite my lip and a mental loophole pops up. "That's a good idea. We could discuss your piano progress over lunch on campus."

"Uh, sure, I guess." He looks a little confused but mostly entertained.

"I'm free after one."

"Awesome." His smile is somehow brighter now

that it's dark. "Union food court?"

"I'll see you then. And uh, thanks."

"For what?"

"For hanging out with me today. I don't really have friends yet here so…you're the first!"

In the shadow, it's hard to read his face, but a moment later, he says, "I'm honored, Wei."

I wave and turn on my heel. As I walk to the bus stop, I try to ignore the fuzzy feeling in my stomach I get whenever he says my name.

This is *not* a date. It's on campus, and you're only going to be talking about class work. With a student. Who is about your age. And incredibly hot and charming.

Why are my palms so sweaty?

I sit and wait in a corner of the Student Union Food Court with a slice of pizza on my tray. Several students are around, but no one seems to pay any attention to me. While I wait, I ponder the ethical ramifications of kissing Logan again. I know he's my student, but there's something growing between us. At the same time, I can't lose my job.

Before I can have another inner crisis, I spot a potential solution; one of the other students from my lecture is walking by me with a tray of food. He's a young kid with darker skin who must be taking private lessons with Felipe.

He sees me, and a flash of recognition grows in his eyes. I smile and wave at him and he gets closer.

"Hi!" I say cheerfully.

"Hi, Professor Wong."

"Please, it's Wei. Wanna sit?"

"Um, OK?" He seems legitimately confused. "Were you meeting someone or something?"

"No! I mean, technically yes. You're in Professor Reyes' BMP-111, correct?"

"Yup."

"I think I've seen you in lectures sitting next to Logan."

"Yeah, but how did you—"

"And there he is!" I get up and wave at Logan, who's now walking up to us with his own tray. He's beaming, but his face drops when he sees the undergrad sitting across from me.

"Hey, Paul," he says. He looks like he's trying to solve a puzzle as he sits down next to him.

"Hey, Logan."

"I spotted Paul as I was eating! I recognized him from BMP-111! The more, the merrier, *amiright?*" I know I sound frantic, but I'll do anything to calm my guilt. I am *not* dating my student, even if he's my co-faculty. *No.*

Logan and Paul share a disturbed glance, then look back down at their food.

"So, how do you two know each other?" I ask, grinning for no reason.

"I'm on the soccer team."

"And I make it a point to know all student athletes," Logan adds, taking a bite of his sandwich.

"That's great." I continue to grin and nod. Paul

looks at me like I've lost my mind. Maybe I have. "Do you two have any questions about music theory for me?"

"Umm, nope," Paul says, and Logan shakes his head.

"Great." We eat our food in silence, and the tension is palpable. Logan keeps stealing glances at me like he's waiting for my lead, but I don't know what to say.

Minutes later, after the quietest lunch of all time, I get up to put away my tray. Once I'm done, I turn around to see Logan and Paul deep in conversation.

Walking back, Paul says, "I gotta run to class. Nice hanging out with you, Professor Wei."

"It's just Wei," I mutter as he runs away. When I turn back to Logan, I see he's already quickly gone to put away his tray. I follow him out the door, and he barely looks at me.

"So...that was lunch. It was fun!"

"Yeah," he deadpans. I'm getting cold shoulder vibes from him, but I can't stop.

"Maybe we could do it again sometime?"

"We don't have to."

"Huh?"

"I'm reading you loud and clear, Wei. We don't have to hang out outside of class."

"What do you mean?" I stop, and he turns around.

"Come on." He opens his arms and looks to the sky. "I'm not an idiot. I know you wrangled Paul because you couldn't stand the idea of hanging out with me outside of the Fine Arts building."

"I, uh—"

"It's fine, I can take a hint. We're both adults. I'll take lessons from the other Assistant Professor. It's no big deal."

Before I can respond, he spins on his heel and strides away. Students walk all around me while I'm left standing there, stunned.

This is kind of what I wanted, right? Moral dilemma squashed. So why do I feel like shit?

10: Logan

Scowling, I'm going over the facility maintenance schedule in my office. Everything seems to piss me off, and burying my head in my work isn't helping this time. It's been over a week since that ill-fated lunch with Wei and Paul. I'm disappointed in what transpired, but I can't help but blame myself.

I pushed too hard, too soon. He's technically my professor, for crying out loud. I barely knew him before I asked him out and I knew it was an ethical no-no, but I did it anyway. He used Paul as a third wheel because he didn't want to turn me down in person. I felt like we had a connection, but I guess I was wrong. I suppose I've been out of the game too long.

Most of all, I blame myself for actually having hope. I thought wanting something for the first time in years meant I was ready to move on and be a functioning member of society again.

Maybe I am, but Wei clearly can't stand the idea of dating me. He kissed me, then thought I was straight, then friend-zoned me, hard. I'm not sure how much more of this I can take. During the music lectures, I pointedly avoid his gaze, and I take my weekly lesson with Felipe instead. Now I simply have to ignore him for the rest of the semester.

I lock up for the night and notice a light snowfall. It's the kind of powdery snow that sticks to the ground momentarily but doesn't stay to form ice. I'm glad it probably won't mess up the roads—the idea of snow-induced car accidents makes me nauseous.

I shake my head to clear it of bad memories as I turn on my car. I rub my hands together then start the heater. As I drive out of the lot, I notice a lone figure on the sidewalk. It's so cold. No one should be out and about right now. The lone figure walks to the bus stop and I can tell he's shivering.

"Aw crap," I mutter to myself as I recognize his face. I turn my car around and park right in front of the bus stop. Wei looks shocked when he sees me, but he's still holding himself to prevent frostbite.

I roll down my window. "Late night?"

I can hear his teeth chatter as he nods.

"Come on. Let me give you a ride home."

"I'm...waiting for the b-b-bus," he stammers. He's still rubbing his arms. Poor guy. I may have some animosity toward him right now, but I don't want my colleague to suffer in the cold. If the snow starts to pile on, his situation will only get worse. If anything were to happen to him out here...

"Please, Wei, you're freezing. I promise we'll keep it professional. Just get in here so I can drive you home."

He looks legitimately conflicted. "It's nice and warm," I sing at him.

He finally dashes into my passenger side and I smile

victoriously. I'm not trying to take advantage of him, but it's nice to know I can break through his stubborn will.

As I drive off of campus he holds his hands in front of the vents. He's still shivering, so I turn the heater up.

"Thank you," he says, once his teeth have stopped chattering.

"Don't mention it. You were freezing. I have an extra seat. It's no big deal."

"OK." I feel his guilty eyes on me but I try to ignore them as I stare at the road. Despite the powder snow, it's an easy drive since so few people are out right now.

We ride mostly in silence, other than Wei telling me where his house is. He really isn't too far from me, about five minutes out of my way, right over the bridge on Dugan's Brook. The idea of us being close enough to hang out outside of school, even platonically, causes a stir in my heart—and in my dick.

We finally pull up to his house, and the snow has mostly stopped.

"Thanks, Logan."

"Don't mention it." I'm still not looking him in the eye. I hope he realizes this changes nothing and I still intend to avoid him and his beautiful face.

"I feel like I need to explain myself. For why I was acting so weird at lunch the other day."

I shrug, looking out into the darkness past my windshield. All I can hear is the humming of the engine. "Is hanging out one-on-one with me such a nightmare?"

"It's not that."

"Then what is it?" I turn to him, all my resolve fading. "Wei, I was under the impression we were becoming friends."

"We are! But we're also..." He waves his hands around like he's trying to find the words.

"Co-faculty?"

He drops his hands. "No. Student and teacher. You're one of my first students here at KU and I *need* to keep this job. I'm responsible for your grade, not Reyes. Hanging out one-on-one, it...blurs lines. I don't want either of us to get in trouble just because when I'm around you, I..." I can hear the desperation in his voice. A spark of sympathy hits my chest because I don't want Wei to lose this job. I can tell how much he needs it.

After a moment of quiet, I finally reply. "I get it. But after this semester, we'll only be co-faculty again."

"That is...true."

"I'm also not too far from you, so I'm kind of your neighbor."

"Also true." Even in the dark, I can see the conflict on his face.

"How about this: why don't we treat each other as student and teacher in class, then co-faculty slash neighbors whenever you need a ride? That way, you'll be able to get to campus easier to do your job better. Then after the semester's over..." I purposely let my voice trail off, unsure of what I want to say.

"The bus does kind of suck," he finally replies.

I snicker. "It really does."

"Alright then. I could use a friend." I can hear the smile in his voice. I'll take it.

"I could too. I'll let you go now, though."

"Thanks, Logan." He opens the door and gets out.

"Text me when you want to go to campus!" I say. "I can drive you whenever!"

"Alright." His smile makes his eyes scrunch up; he's beautiful. "Night, man."

"Night!" I beam at him and wait for him to get inside before I drive away.

It figures I finally take a class and nearly end up in a student-teacher conflict of interest. We can't pursue whatever's happening between us, no matter how badly I want to. Friends is good too, though—for now, anyway. For Wei, I'm willing to wait.

11: Wei

The following Sunday, I finally get a chance to catch up on all my errands. I'm sifting through a week's worth of mail in the kitchen and see one letter that puts a frown on my face; it's a spam mail for my aunt who no longer lives here. I put it to the side when Pei and Galen walk in. My nephew is shrugging off his winter coat, and just seeing him makes me smile.

"How was shopping?"

"I got new shoes Uncle Wei! I'm gonna wear them so I can go fast!"

"Maybe tomorrow," Pei chuckles, putting her bags down. "I don't want them getting dirty before you even get to school."

"OK," Galen says. "Uncle Wei, wanna go outside with me? The snow's all melted and I wanna play soccer!"

"Um, I'm really busy paying these bills," I reply, looking back down.

"Alright," he says, sounding defeated the way only a seven-year-old can.

I look up and notice the frown on his face as he stares longingly out the window.

"Hey, kiddo." He turns to look at me. "I'll be done soon. We can go play for a little bit, but I need to talk to your mom first."

"OK!" He sounds so joyous. I think I just made his day.

"Go use the bathroom first then change into your muddy shoes." Pei pats him on the back and he runs off. She looks down at the letter that's addressed to our aunt. "Why is she still getting letters here?"

"Spam." I shrug. Our aunt was our legal guardian and our only family, but she left us years ago to fend for ourselves. I don't really want to think about her because when I do, I get upset. While she supported us financially, she always felt emotionally closed off. As a child, I wondered why we never felt like a close-knit family, and it hurt. So, I block out the memories of her. All I can do is focus on the future, being a great parental figure, and supporting my nephew. "I'm going to pay the heating bill online."

"This is a lot," she says, looking at the paper in my hands. "I can pay it this time."

"No, I got this. You had to buy groceries and clothes for Galen." I stand up. "The money's finally coming in from my new job. That's on top of my catering gig."

"Alright." She looks unconvinced but drops the subject. "How's it been at KU? You like being a music teacher?"

"Living the dream!" I nod at her, then walk down the stairs to my room to go pay some bills.

{

Today, I am not living the dream. It's Monday, and I'm in my office trying to practice the harp, but I keep messing up my fingering patterns. My mind keeps going back to seeing Logan in class today. I hadn't texted him for a ride, and as I taught my first lecture on sharps and flats, I felt him staring at me. This time, though, his eyes didn't have the sparkle I've gotten so accustomed to. He watched me with a sterile, hollow gaze.

I'd wanted us to be student and teacher only—well, I got my fucking wish.

After messing up another note, I grunt in frustration and push the harp back upright on its stand. I get up and pace around my office, shaking my hands. My heart beats extra fast when Logan's around, but when he keeps his distance, I still can't focus. What's wrong with me?

The answer to my rhetorical questions emerges from the dark corners of my mind: I'm drawn to Logan. I want to spend time with him. I want to get to know him and see if I can bring back that prince-charming-type guy I met at the Athletics Center those weeks ago.

The Center...*that's it!* I check my phone and look up the Athletics Center's hours. Apparently, there are designated faculty hours in the state-of-the-art fitness center. Maybe...I really need to exercise. Like, right now.

Walking into the fitness room, I realize I'm out of my

depth. I don't know how to use any of these machines. I left physical education behind in high school, and that was over ten years ago. Logan isn't around either, so my genius plan might not be so smart after all. There's hardly anyone here, but I need to create the illusion I'm working out so I can accidentally-but-actually-on-purpose bump into Logan. I put my coat down and choose a machine that looks simple enough to use.

I sit down and put my arms at both sides where giant metal poles reach down around me. I push forward on the metal poles, but to no avail. I try again, really straining myself, and the weights don't move. I know I'm out of shape, but this is a little ridiculous; I expected it to budge at least a little! I try one more time, really grunting, when a voice breaks me out of my fruitless endeavor.

"I don't want you to hurt yourself." I turn to my right to see Logan, arms crossed and an easy smirk on his face. He looks so unimpressed, but in his KU faculty uniform—a simple gray short-sleeved polo with our school emblem—he looks damn good.

"Uh…" I look around and see no one's nearby. "No pain, no gain?"

He's fighting a smile and I'll take that as a win. "You won't get any gain, just pain, if you continue on this track." He leans on the machine. "You're sitting backward and pushing the machine the wrong way."

I feel like an idiot and immediately get up and rotate.

"So what brings you here?"

"I thought…It said on the website it's faculty-only hours."

"Yes, but what brings *you* here?" He sounds so cocky. I know he's patronizing me, but it's kind of flirty and hot.

"Thought I'd exercise?"

"Uh-huh." He's not buying it.

"And maybe I wanted to hang out with you." His eyebrows jump. "To learn! How to use these machines. And I figured you could teach me."

"Co-faculty to co-faculty?"

"Exactly! We're not in my music lecture so..." I shrug pleadingly, looking into his warm eyes.

"Right." He seems to still be pondering my intentions.

"And afterwards I could use a ride home...from a neighbor?"

He smiles and nods. "Well, alright then." He seems to accept my shallow premise to hang out, and I try to bite back a smile.

He leans in, and, for a moment, I contemplate kissing him. Instead, he moves a lever on the machine, presumably to adjust the resistance. "Let's get you exercising, *Assistant Professor Wong.*"

The deep tenor of his voice saying my name once again gives me chills.

12: Logan

I pull the massive bar back onto the rack and Wei lets go. "Good job," I say.

He sits up on the bench and groans. "What are the chances I won't be sore tomorrow?"

"Zero percent." I smirk. I convinced Wei to switch to some bench presses with me for the past twenty minutes. I don't have the heart to tell him I barely put any weights on the bar he's been struggling with.

"Getting old sucks."

I laugh. "Dude, you're what, twenty-five?"

"Twenty-nine, but thank you."

"I'm twenty-seven. If you're old, I'm old."

He smiles at me, and I try to ignore the beads of sweat coming down his forehead. They trace his neckline and flow beneath his shirt. I wonder what he'd look like without a top...

I clear my throat. "I think that's enough for today. Let me get you a towel." I leave to go to the locker room area and get a supply of fresh towels. I need to move around to clear my head of naughty thoughts of Wei—of him sweaty, or lying underneath me at the bench press, or taking off his clothes at my gym...

Nope. Don't go down that road. He's your professor and only wants to be friends. *Bad horny thoughts, bad.*

When I return, towel in hand, I hear her voice before I see her.

"Look at you!" Professor Hark is standing in front of Wei, clad in tight workout clothes with a bright pink sweatband on her head. "I'd make a pact with the devil to have a tight core like that."

"I don't eat much." He looks so uncomfortable; I need to save him.

"Here you are, Wei." I hand him a towel. "I see you've met Professor Hark."

"Logie, my dear, where have you been hiding your friend here?" She puts her hand on his elbow, and I grit my teeth. I may not date much, but I know that maneuver.

"He's new to KU."

"I'm Wei."

"Very nice to meet you." she says.

"I'm closing up soon, Professor Hark." I reply.

"Oh, I won't take long." She grins at Wei and starts stretching her arms above her. "Gotta get in some squats before I go home. You know, Logan and I go way back."

"Really?" Wei asks. I try to subtly shake my head at him.

"Oh yeah. I've been trying to get him to make an honest woman out of me since I started working here two years ago." She grabs a small weight and starts doing squats in front of us, as if it's a normal thing for people to do when talking. "A tall broad-shouldered man like him? Who wouldn't wanna lock him down?"

"Who wouldn't indeed." Wei, to his credit, just sounds amused.

"Alright, well, this has been fun!" I interject. "Um..."

"I promise I'll be done soon, Logie!" She beams at me and my eyes have no choice but to follow her up and down as she squats.

"I'll meet you upstairs," Wei says, wiping his brow. "Nice meeting you, Professor Hark."

"It's Aggie!" She looks at the ceiling and doesn't stop squatting. "And seven...and eight...and nine. Ooh it burns!"

After Wei leaves, Hark stands up straight and looks at me. "He seems nice."

My face gets warmer. "He's...co-faculty."

"So am I." Her tone suggests something I don't care to interpret. She winks and walks over to get another weight and I use that as my excuse to leave and start locking up.

Wei and I spend the next few days falling into somewhat of a groove. We text on occasion, usually to coordinate rides. Sometimes he meets me to exercise, and other days he says he gets a ride from his sister. Our commutes feel like the most natural thing in the world. Talking to him about my day doesn't feel uncomfortable at all. He doesn't judge me for being a college dropout who doesn't know anything about music. When I get Wei talking about performing, he gets so vibrant and passionate that I have to try hard not to stare into his eyes while I'm on the road.

He and I are student and teacher, co-faculty, and neighbors, but there's this undercurrent that we're so much more than that. We haven't really addressed the massive elephant in the room that was born underneath the mistletoe at the formal. We're getting along well, though, so I don't want to mess it up by bringing up that clandestine kiss.

Speaking of secrets, one day during the athlete practice hour, I notice one of the men's soccer players has a hickey on his neck that he really doesn't want his friends to know about. College kids—they never change. I help him out by discreetly giving him a towel to wrap around his neck and he thanks me. Afterward, I continue on with my day, working to keep my baby the Athletics Center, clean and functional.

In the men's locker room, that same player walks up to me, his jacket noticeably pulled up to his neck.

"Hey Logan. Thanks for the um…" He points to the towel I gave him to hide the mark on his neck. He puts it in my linen cart and I smirk at him.

"No problem, Landee." I enjoy casually chatting with the student athletes. They're good kids, and when we talk, it's a distraction that puts me at ease.

"You know my real name?"

"I know everything about the athletes. But your secrets are safe with me, young one." The team only knows him by his last name, Landon. "I assume you had a date last night that you don't want the guys to know about?"

"Um…"

"I recall you talking about girls nonstop last semester."

"Well, I'm trying something new." Huh? "I mean…personality-wise!" Oh, he's queer, too.

I stare at him confused. "Landon, isn't your best friend dating a guy?"

"Uh…"

"No one should be ashamed of whom they're dating. Your friends will accept you, I'm sure." There's my trademark moment of wisdom that I regularly share with these kids. In actuality, I don't have many friends and certainly don't date. Of course, there's one person who could solve both of those problems.

"It's…all just new," Landon says.

"Fair enough."

"Thanks, though." Right before he leaves, he turns to me. "Hey, Logan? How do you know if someone… likes you? And wants to date you?"

Aw shit. Isn't that the million-dollar question? I think about Wei's beautiful face and our car rides together.

"Considering what's going on in my life, I am *not* the person you should be asking."

"Oh," he replies. *Crap, I can't believe I said that out loud.* I try to muster up some semblance of real-world advice.

"But, I will tell you this: nothing will change unless you keep hanging out with him. Or her. Whoever." That seems to appease him as he leaves with a smile.

As I lock up, my mind drifts to Wei, how he runs hot and cold with me. I can never tell if he wants me to make a move or not. Not a day goes by that I don't think about him kissing my cheek at Christmas.

I hope Landon works out his relationship woes. I hope I work out mine as well.

13: Wei

I'm setting up my music to practice the harp in my office when there's a knock at the door. I smile before opening it, confident I know who it is.

"Hey!" I'm greeted with Logan's massive smile and shining brown eyes.

"Hey yourself! To what do I owe this visit?" I don't wait for an answer before letting him in. If that's a metaphor for how I feel about him, I refuse to interpret it.

"So I got you some snacks. You told me you don't eat enough, and now that we're working out together, I'd be the worst workout buddy ever if I didn't provide you with the right sustenance." He sits down on the chair opposite my instrument and shucks off his backpack. Rummaging inside it, he says, "I've got turkey jerky, canned tuna, and lots of different brands of trail mix."

He takes out the plastic bag filled with goodies. "I actually haven't even had these, so I figured we could try them together."

"That's so generous of you Logan." I sit across from him

and lean on my knees. "But if Reyes catches you eating here, she'll have your head, then mine."

He chuckles. "What are you up to now?"

"About to practice." I tap the soundboard of the harp. "Then I have Queer Pride Union later."

"Oh, that's right."

"Yeah, I'm the faculty advisor. Sometimes I run 'Safe Space' where I give confidential advice to kids in need."

"That's really admirable," he replies. "So no working out today?"

"No, sorry, my sister is picking me up after."

"It's cool. There's a soccer game today, so I usually clean up after."

We both nod in silence; it's an awkward ten seconds.

"So..." he says. "I don't wanna, um, keep you from playing." He zips up his backpack and my heart beats a little faster.

"You can stay if you want," I blurt out, before my mind registers what I'm saying.

His eyebrows jump. "Uh, sure!"

"Alright." My face gets warmer as I pull the instrument closer to me. "I'm still not that good so..."

"I enjoy hearing you play, regardless." His words make my heart beat a little faster, but I focus and put my fingers on the strings. I don't know what Logan and I are doing, but somewhere deep down, I don't want it to end.

67

The Queer Pride Union room is this massive loft tucked away on the top floor of the Student Union building. I walk in and unlock the door and turn on the lights. The safe sex paraphernalia and pride posters on the wall bring a smile to my face. It's good to know this generation will have an easier time coming out than the last.

I sit down at the desk and boot up my PC to get some work done. Not too many people come to 'Safe Space' office hours, but, of the few who have, I can tell they needed it. It feels good knowing I'm making a difference in their lives.

Today, the first person to come through is Dane, the vice president. He seems flustered, and I realize he needs some confidential advice. Being as this is 'Safe Space,' I let him talk. He gives me this massive monologue about how he has a crush on a soccer player but doesn't know if his crush likes him back. I calmly recommend he goes to see him at the game happening right now, and Dane looks visibly relieved.

"Thanks, Wei. Hopefully we can chat and see where things go."

"Remember, making assumptions in your head won't help the situation. It sounds scary, but you should really consider talking things out with him. Let him know your concerns and how you feel about him." Hearing the words come out of my mouth makes me realize something: I've been stringing Logan along. We haven't addressed the kiss from Christmas, and try as I might to resist, I'm starting to have feelings for him.

"I need to take my own advice," I mutter, taking out my phone to text Logan.

Wei: *What are you doing Saturday?*

Logan: *I work Saturday evenings, closing up the Facility.*

Logan: *Y?*

Wei: *Thought I'd swing by, get some practicing done, then after, get my exercise on.*

Wei: *And maybe get a ride home from u? If that's cool.*

Logan: *Of course neighbor!*

Wei: (smiley face emoji)

14: Logan

"You really held your own today on the weights. I'm proud of you." I hold the door open to the locker room and Wei walks through.

"I'm still going to be sore all over tomorrow, aren't I?" He's smirking at me, sweat dripping down his brow.

"Eh...probably." I shrug and he smiles back.

"Ass." He chuckles and sits down on a bench. I realize how alone we really are. Barely any staff exercises here on Saturdays, but I still need to keep the facilities operating—again, I'm essentially married to my job.

"You've got a potty mouth, Assistant Professor Wong."

"Well, I have this friend who keeps my arms and chest burning at the gym, Mr. Micucci." He makes a faux-angry face at me. It's adorable.

"And so dramatic." I laugh.

"I'll remember that when I grade your next music quiz."

That's right; he's still my professor for the next two months. I almost forgot today while we were working out as friends. Now we're flirting in the locker room, and I have no clue if I should make a move or not.

"Um…I should go shower."

"Right," I reply, nodding rapidly. "I think we're the only ones left here on a Saturday night. So I should…go. Lock up and all that." Why is my heart beating so fast?

"Sure. Meet you upstairs?" Wei stands up, turns around, and—good Lord—takes his shirt off right in front of me. My throat goes dry as I stare at the world of smooth skin on Wei's back.

"Uh…uh…yeah." He turns and looks at me, putting his fingers into his shorts and I spin around so quickly my head hurts. Rushing out the door, I breathe in through my nose to catch my breath. *Do not watch your new friend slash neighbor slash professor in the shower, Logan.* That's wrong on like a hundred levels.

I'm spared more temptation as Wei joins me, fully dressed, after I'm almost done locking up. We get to my car in the cold winter air, the campus sky pitch black even though it's not even eight. Buckling up, I notice the occasional snowflake floating onto my windshield. I haven't checked the weather recently, so I didn't know it was going to snow.

Twenty minutes later, Wei and I are laughing, swapping stories about our lives while I breeze down the highway.

"And he wanted me to be a teacher at his school!"

"That's adorable." I chuckle. "You're really close to your nephew. That's great."

"Well, I'm kind of his father figure."

"I think it's incredible that you care about your family so much. You're...you're really something, Wei." I smile and turn to him. He's already grinning at me.

There's this quiet moment, and I take in how beautiful he is. Past him out the window, however, I see the snow is now falling down hard. How have I not noticed while driving this whole time?

Fortunately, we're approaching the bridge across Dugan's Brook, meaning we should be at Wei's house soon. I just want to get home and off the road, but since the snow is starting to whip up and my visibility is lowered, I'm forced to slow down.

I think I'm in the clear across the bridge when an approaching car on the other side slides, rotating so it's nearly perpendicular to the rails—and us.

"Shit!" I shout. I brake hard and turn the wheel completely to the right. Because of the blizzard-like conditions outside, my car ends up sliding as well and not stopping. We swerve as I try to regain control. Snow whips around us.

My car misses the other vehicle by mere inches. Instead, we swerve to our right and I graze the metal wall of the bridge overlooking the brook.

"Fuck!" Wei yells, bracing himself for impact. These ten seconds seem to span out forever, but then I do finally feel the car gain traction again. After what felt like eternity, we're back to moving slowly in a straight path, not touching the wall or anything.

"Woah," Wei says. "That was a close one. Don't wanna

take a swim in Dugan's Brook, now, do we?"

"Are you hurt?" I ask, driving to Wei's house on autopilot.

"No. It was just a bit scary. I don't drive often, so I'm not used to it. You probably go through this kind of weather all the time, right?"

Shit.

I almost drove off the bridge.

Fuck.

I tell myself to breathe slowly, to get my heart rate to calm down, but nothing's helping. My breathing is rapid and shallow. All I see is snow — the snow that took my parents' lives. I see the wrecked car, the one that fell in the water, the one police asked me to identify.

I see their graves.

Wei is talking to me, but all I hear is the police officer at my door telling me there's been an accident. I hear the funeral procession. I hear the lawyers telling me how much money and assets I have now.

It's the present day, but I feel like I'm twenty-one years old again and my parents are gone. I'm an orphan and I have no family.

I don't know how long it's been, but I think we've parked in front of Wei's house. He's still talking, waving his hands in front of me. I think I've shut off the car, and maybe Wei is putting his hand on my shoulder. I don't know for sure.

The snow.

The accident.

My parents.

Driving off a bridge.

You're Logan Micucci, right?

There's been an accident, son.

I'm so sorry.

I shiver as the tears fall down my face and I curl into the steering wheel.

"Logan?" I hear a voice ask.

"My parents. They…they died in a car accident on a snowy night like this."

"*What?*"

"There was a lot of ice and…they lost control. D-D-Drove off a bridge. Just like we almost did." I sniff and shiver as the tears continue to cascade off my face. "We almost died t-t-too. I a-almost lost you, Wei."

I sense Wei getting up and leaving, closing the passenger door. Good. I don't want him to see me like this.

I can't keep pretending everything is fine. Wei doesn't need someone broken in his life like me. I'm just going to sit here until the pain goes away, then I'll drive off. I'll go home alone where I can cry and be broken in peace.

I hear my car door open. Looking up, I see the face of an angel in the snow. No, it's someone I know.

"Come on," Wei says, his voice warm like a candle in a storm. "You're coming inside with me. We'll get you settled."

I let him pull me out of the car and into the blistering cold. He holds me up while we walk.

15: Wei

"Let's get those shoes off you." I bend down, untie the laces, and Logan pulls his feet out, all while leaning against the wall. "My room is down here. Are you able to go down the stairs?"

He gives me a feeble nod and I'll have to trust him since there's not enough room for me to hold him while we go down. He leans on the rail and makes it to the basement area that's been converted into my room.

Past the laundry machine, I unlock the door and Logan follows me. Once inside, I carefully tell him to take off his coat and lead him to the bed. He's wearing outside clothes on my clean sheets, but I don't care—he needs me. Hearing him confess that his parents died on a snowy night like this broke my heart. I know he's going through a fugue state of post-trauma because he barely noticed when I was talking to him.

I can't let him be alone right now; he's someone I've come to care for deeply, even if we're just friends.

So I sit next to him on the bed and lean his head onto my shoulder. It's not long before he lies on my lap and shivers and sobs. I don't mind his tears are on me; if I'd known my parents for years before I lost them, I'd probably be like him too. The idea of losing my sister or nephew to a force of nature is not a pretty one.

"I-I-I've been alone this whole time. I don't have any other family."

"It's alright," I whisper.

"I hate that they left me alone. I h-h-hate it so much."

"I know." I rub his back and let him cry. This certainly explains a lot about him. He spends long nights at work, married to his job. Logan's smiles usually have moments where they falter. I can only imagine him holding himself up for so long, feeling alone. I had tough times growing up, but at least Pei and I had each other.

"I don't...I don't even know how to function without them. I can't...I don't have anyone to—"

"It's OK. You don't have to say anything." I rub his back some more and the shivering dies down. "I'm here, Logan." I hope he knows I mean it. I hold him in my lap until I hear him fall asleep, then gently move so I can get up.

A while later, I'm dressed in my pajamas eating some soup when I hear Logan stirring. I swivel in the chair, noodles hanging out of my mouth, to see him slowly getting up.

"Mm...How long was I asleep?" he mumbles.

"About an hour." I put down my bowl and stand up in front of him. "Are you hungry? It's pretty late, but you should eat."

"Mm...OK." He's still not making eye contact, but I guide him up the stairs. I'm thankful that Pei and Galen are already asleep. I lead him to our small kitchen and dining area where a bowl of ramen is waiting for him.

I sit him down and give him a spoon, and he immediately digs in—I guess he was hungry. I'm glad to see it's still warm, but not too hot that it burns him. He looks adorable with his messed-up bed head. I almost smile until I remember how we got here.

"Glad you like it."

"I love it," he mumbles through mouthfuls of noodles. He's like a big puppy, gobbling up all this food. He probably hasn't eaten in six hours or so.

"And after you're done, you can take as much time as you need before you go home."

He freezes at this and finally makes eye contact with me. "You're right. I...should be good to go...soon."

Seeing him hurting, I don't even realize it when I say the next five words: "Unless you'd like to stay."

Logan looks startled for a moment, then looks back down at the bowl. "Are you sure? I don't mean to impose," he says, slowly scooping up more soup with his spoon. He seems so small and defeated. In that moment, it's like I'm seeing the side of Logan that no one else sees. Screw being his professor. He's my friend, and I think he needs me. I need to take care of him tonight.

"It's no problem at all." I smile look into his eyes; I hope he knows I mean it. "I'll go get you an extra toothbrush so you can wash up." His mouth briefly curves into a small smile, and I take that for a win.

Once we're both washed up, we're back in my room getting ready for bed. Logan takes off his pants, and I have to look at the ceiling to not ogle his long, thick legs in tiny, black boxer-briefs. *The ceiling looks lovely, lalala...*

"Thank you, Wei." He wipes his eyes and curls up in my blanket. It's dawning on me that this is the first time I've taken a guy back to my bed—ironic, considering how sex-less this is going to be.

"Again, it's not a problem." I nod at him and notice his brown eyes twinkle at me. I shift my weight left and right, then softly clap my hands. "Well, I'll be upstairs on the couch if you need me."

"Wait, what?" Logan looks shocked and horrified. "You're not gonna sleep here with me?"

"Uh..." I try to find the words to respond, but I'm coming up blank. *Run away, Wei. This is a massive breach of the friend-zone deal you made.*

"Of course," he says, looking down, heartbroken. "I'm sorry, that would be crossing...I mean, you're still my professor..."

"Um..."

"Fuck, I wish you weren't, though." He closes his eyes. "I didn't want to be alone, for once."

"Then, I'll stay." The words leave my mouth before I can stop them.

"What?"

"It's my bed...so I'll stay." I click off the light and crawl under the covers with Logan. My queen-size mattress is just big enough to give us both space, yet Logan is so close to me, only inches away. I swear I can hear his heartbeat. "Did you want to talk about your parents some more?"

"I...I just..." He sounds so small, so hurt. Everything about tonight is so fucked up, but I can't leave Logan's side. He moves towards me, and I pull him close, bridging the gap between us, unable to fight what's been happening with us, not tonight.

"I just miss them," he murmurs into my neck. I rub him with my right arm as he curls into me further. "I thought I was over it, but tonight when we almost drove off the road..."

"It's OK, I got you." I gently rub his back as he sobs in my arms, and sleep eventually overtakes us.

16: Logan

I wake up in a bed that isn't mine, with no memory of how I got here. As I stretch, I notice I'm still wearing my work polo. Weird.

I feel a warm indent in the pillow next to mine; someone was just here. I breathe in and recognize the scent. Wei was sleeping here?

Of course, now I recall; I'm at Wei's house. I dropped him off, then I...I think he let me sleep over?

Shit, I don't think we had sex. Right?

"No, no we didn't," I mutter to myself as I put my slacks back on.

I walk up the stairs to the sound of cartoons, pots, and pans. It's music to my ears—typically I wake up to the void of silence at home or, hell, even when I sleep at work.

Opening the door at the top of the stairs, I see a little Asian kid at the table. He's got a bowl of cereal and a tablet in front of him blasting cartoons.

"Who are you?" he asks, loudly.

I'm saved from answering by the gorgeous man

standing by the stove. "He's...my friend. The one I told you stayed overnight because he *wasn't feeling* well?" His eyebrows bounce as he looks at the slender woman by the counter, presumably his sister.

"Oh right," the woman by the counter replies, pulling out mugs. She looks at Wei, then at me. "Uh..."

"I didn't know you had friends, Uncle Wei," the kid says with a mouthful of cereal.

"Don't talk with your mouth full, sweetie." The woman in scrubs, presumably his mom, sits down next to the kid. "Your uncle is allowed to have friends."

"Hi everyone," I announce, uncomfortably.

"Have a seat. I'm making omelets," Wei says, smiling. I do as I'm told, and I'm sitting close to the woman who's pointedly looking at the ceiling. "This is Logan. Logan, this is my sister and nephew."

"I'm Penny," she says, finally looking at me, smiling. "Pei, or Penny, whatever's easiest."

"I'm Galen. That's 'Gal,' then 'en.' Some people say 'Gayl-en' but that's wrong."

I chuckle at the kid. I don't spend much time around little ones, so I'm taken aback by how candid he is. It's so cute. "Well I'm 'Loag,' then 'en' and I'm glad no one calls me 'Logg-En.'"

Pei and Galen giggle, and it's good to know they're not 100 percent uncomfortable around me.

Wei serves us delicious omelets and we three adults make small talk about my job at KU. After a bit, Pei says she needs to go to work, so she kisses Galen goodbye and bids us all farewell. Wei tells his nephew to go brush his teeth while he cleans up.

"I should probably get some work done," Wei

says while washing the dishes. "I bet you have a lot to do, too."

"Not really." I shrug. "And thanks again...for..."

"Don't mention it." He smiles, but I know what he's not saying; he could lose his job if anyone finds out about last night.

"Truthfully, I barely remember last night. The last clear memory I have is of us driving home and—"

"You were in shock. Traumatic memories. No need to talk about it." Wei dries his hands and leans on the counter. "I did what any friend would do."

"Yeah, but it's more than that, isn't it?" Wei's expression becomes serious. "I don't remember last night, but this morning, it was like...like a weight had lifted off my shoulders."

"Logan..."

"Wei, I know you're technically still my professor, but I need to know—"

"Uncle Wei!" Galen comes barging in. "Can we go outside and play football? I want to use my new snow boots and play sports in the snow like the players I watched online!"

"Oh, kiddo, you know I'm not really good at sports. And I should get some schoolwork done. I'm sure you can toss the ball around by yourself."

"But it's boring to toss it around by myself," he whines. He looks down and pouts at his uncle. Poor kid. This inspires me to say something bold.

"You know, I'm a bit of an athlete myself."

"Really?" Galen beams up at me, his voice filled with hope.

"I could toss around the old pigskin with you if

you want." I smile at him.

"I don't want pigskin. I wanna play football!"

"That's what I mean!" I beam right back at him, then turn serious as I look at Wei. "If that's OK with your uncle."

"Pleaseohpleaseohplease?!" Galen bobs up and down.

Wei looks up at me, wincing. "You don't have to. I'm sure you have a million things to do, Logan."

"Not really." I shrug. "I could throw the ball around for an hour or so. And if you're not too busy, you can watch us."

A smile slowly creeps on his face, then he looks down at Galen. "Go get your coat."

"Yes!"

"And say thank you to Logan."

"Thank you, Logan!" His little voice echoes through the hall as he runs to the closet.

17: Wei

Is "fatherly-vibes" a kink? Because if so, I'm totally there. I'm standing at the living room window, sipping coffee and watching Galen and Logan play some form of football outside. I knew Logan was physically attractive. I thought of him as flirtatious, fun, generous, and vulnerable. But now? I'm watching him teach Galen how to throw what I think is a spiral, and he's being so supportive to my nephew. It's almost like they're father and son, and Galen is having so much fun with him.

Fuck, that is *hot*. Alright, him being a caring, dad-type of guy is *definitely* a kink.

Ninety minutes later—how neither of them collapsed is beyond me—they're both coming inside, laughing.

"And that's called a touchdown dance!" Logan chuckles.

"Wow!" Galen replies, shucking off his shoes.

"OK, put your coat away and go watch TV. Then

we're going to eat lunch." I announce.

"Logan are you going to have lunch with us? I have dinosaur chicken nuggets."

Logan throws his head back and laughs while I smile. "I'm sure Logan is busy."

"I do have a few things to do at home," he says, tears of laughter in his eyes. This is a major improvement from last night, and it's great to see Galen getting along well with him. "But hey, maybe we can play again some time."

"Can you teach me how to play soccer?"

"Maybe. Better yet, you can meet real college soccer players. They can teach you techniques, and you can watch their game at our school." He looks up at me. "If your uncle and mom say it's OK."

At this, I swear Galen's eyes turn into giant saucers. "A real soccer game? Wow! Canwecanwecanwe?"

I chuckle. "You behave this week and we'll talk about it. Now go get ready."

"OK. Thanks, Logan!" His little feet pitter-patter down the hallway.

"Thank you. For spending the morning with him."

"He's great," Logan says, grinning. I walk with him out the door.

"Well, it means a lot that a big virile man like yourself can show him stuff I never could."

"Virile, huh?" His voice is once again dripping with innuendo. Good to know Logan's back.

"You know what I mean. The kid is energetic and loves sports, and I was always the artsy kid. I actually liked my piano lessons, but so far Galen has no interest in music."

"Maybe he'll come around." We walk to his car, and he

turns to me. Even in the cold, simply looking at Logan warms me up. "In the meantime, I could come play some more football with him next week. And later down the line, he could meet the soccer boys at the U and learn some things if you and Penny agree to that. Lord knows those undergrads owe me a favor or two."

"That sounds nice. For sure. Thank you, Logan."

"I owe you a thousand favors as well, especially after last night, so thank *you*, Wei."

"I did…what any friend or neighbor would do." I fight the urge to reach up and kiss his beautiful face. "I gotta go though. I'll text you if I need a ride this week. You sure you're alright?"

He nods and looks at me, a quiet spark passing through us. "I am now, thanks to you."

On Thursday, after my last lesson, I get to my office in time to see Logan striding up to me, beaming.

"Assistant Professor Wong."

"Mr. Micucci." I grin at him.

"I think we're way past that considering we're…" He walks inside and I pause to look at him. "Co-faculty."

"And neighbors," I add, setting up my sheet music. "Do you have any questions about this week's lecture?"

"Did you give me a hundred on my quiz?" I can hear him grinning.

"You know I can't answer that." I'm rolling my eyes as I sit down in front of the harp.

"Then no questions. I just locked up the Athletics Center for the night, thought I'd see if you wanted a ride."

"I was going to get some practicing done."

"Perfect. I love hearing you play."

Before I can retort, the one question that's been on my mind since last Saturday bubbles up. I bite my lip, then ask, "Are you sure you're OK? After last weekend."

"I'm fine."

"Logan." I look him in the eye. "You were in, like, a dissociative state. You told me all about your parents. I don't blame you for being distraught, no matter how long it's been."

"I told you I'm fine." He looks serious, but I'm not sure I believe him.

"Alright." I decide to drop it. "But if you ever need anyone to talk to…I'm here. And there's also counseling on campus."

"Do you really want to make me feel better?" I nod, almost afraid to let him continue. If he asks for a kiss or to sleep over again, I'd probably let him, and that thought is terrifying. "I'd like to hear you play those strings."

My eyebrows jump. *Is he serious?*

"I'm serious," he continues, reading my mind. "Hearing you perform, whether it's a piano piece or just scales on the harp, it…" He looks down, trying to find the words. "It calms me down. Like last Saturday, it's you…You calm me down, Wei."

My heart is beating so fast and I bet my face is beet red. I nod, unable to speak. I start to play some rudimentary melodies on the harp and Logan's posture visibly relaxes in the chair. His head is tilted back, and he stares at the ceiling. I focus on where to put my fingers on the strings, anything to drown out what Logan just said. I think about rhythms and try not to dwell on all the lines he and I have been crossing everyday.

18: Logan

Playing football with Wei's nephew was such fun. The kid is so full of life, and it gives me even more of an excuse to see his sexy uncle. While we ignore each other in class, he comes to the gym some nights and gets a ride home with me. Luckily, there are no more mental breakdowns on my part. Some afternoons I go to his office and listen to him practice the harp. The angelic symbolism of a beautiful man playing this particular instrument is not lost upon me.

With all our car rides and quiet moments, we don't talk about anything serious. He's still my professor, and I'm still his student, though also co-faculty. We don't bring up our mistletoe kiss or anything meaningful like that, yet the undercurrent of tension is always there. It's difficult to believe my feelings are one-sided, not with the way he looks at me. Still, we can't do anything about it; like a cartoon coyote running off a cliff not realizing he's out of ledge, we are choosing not to look down, lest we fall. I think I already am...

A few weeks later, I ask the men's soccer team if anyone is willing to teach a seven-year-old all about soccer drills. Ravi and Kareem agree, and, because they're a four-man unit, Omar and Landon volunteer to help as well.

Wei, Galen, and I approach the field where the boys are already waiting for us on this surprisingly sunny Saturday morning. There are some cones, a net, and a couple of balls on the ground. Galen clings to Wei's side, but I'm sure he'll warm up to these knuckleheads in no time.

"Morning, boys!" I holler, walking over to them.

"Logan!" Landon and Omar reply, with Ravi and Kareem simply waving.

"Boys, meet Galen." Galen gives a limp wave but is still hiding behind Wei. "Meet the soccer boys, Ravi, Kareem, Landon, and Omar. And do you guys know Professor Wong?"

"Wei, hi," Ravi says.

"We uh, know each other," Landon says. There's a story there, I can hear it in his voice, but for now, I'll let it go.

Ravi bends down to look Galen in the eye. "Hey little man, we heard you like soccer."

Galen nods, and Kareem walks up to Ravi. "What do you think, Ravi? Do we have a future Messi on our hands?" He points to Galen, and the little boy beams at Kareem.

"There's only one way to find out." Ravi grins and kicks a ball in the air and bounces it on his knees a few times with ease, then lowers it back down. "You wanna learn some drills, little man?"

Galen looks up at Wei, and his uncle smiles. "Go on."

Galen runs up to them, and the last thing I hear him say is "I'm gonna be better than Messi!" The four guys howl with laughter and proceed to show him some drills.

Wei and I sit down on a nearby bench and watch. "I really appreciate you doing this, Logan."

I shrug. "Like I said, these boys owe me." We're talking out of earshot, but occasionally Omar eyes us, suspiciously. *We're not doing anything wrong. We're just co-faculty. And neighbors. And friends...*

"I think you made Galen's whole year with this. My sister and I barely play sports with him, and we can't really afford lessons from real coaches."

"His dad's not in the picture?"

Wei shakes his head. "She said it was a short-lived relationship, and I try not to pry. I don't need to hear about my sister's sex life."

I smile. "What about grandparents? Uncles, cousins?"

"It's only Pei and me."

I sigh and look down. "Losing parents is the worst."

"Actually, neither of us remembers our parents. They died when we were young. My aunt had no choice but to take us in."

"You have an aunt?"

Wei pauses and kicks some grass with his shoe. "She moved away before Galen was born. She was always emotionally distant, anyway. So if you see my Aunt Lynette on the street, tell her we're fine without her." He chuckles like it's a joke, but I know all too well about deflecting stories about your family. "I just hope we're raising Galen right. Some days, I don't know..." He hangs his head.

"Hey, you're doing an amazing job." I put my hand on his wrist. I want to take his pain away, to take care of him the way he did for me. "You're an incredible uncle and father figure for him. That kid is so loved. He's lucky to have a mom and uncle like you two."

He looks up at me, eyes welling up. "You think so?" Fuck, I want to kiss him so badly.

In the distance I hear Kareem and Ravi yell "Goalllll!" and I look up to see Galen running circles around them, laughing. Off to the side, Landon and Omar are grinning at us, and I immediately drop my hand. *Shit.*

After the Wong family has gone home, I'm putting away the cones and other supplies in a utility closet. Once I lock up, I see the soccer boys waiting in the hallway, and Omar is grinning wildly.

"Thanks again guys," I say, trying to ignore their stares. I expect them to leave, but they just stand there taking me in. My pulse starts to race. "Can I help you?"

"This is your plan, you guys. I'm out of here," Kareem mutters, shaking his head. He leaves, and I'm left with three jocks instead of four.

Ravi clears his throat. "Galen is a good kid. And that Wei guy is uh…He's cool."

Omar hops up and down. "And you two look *so* cute together!" he squeals. "I'm sorry. I couldn't hold it in anymore." Ravi and Landon roll their eyes, and my face gets warm.

"OK, I'm locking up now." I turn my heel and head up the stairs.

"Look, I know him from QPU. He's a good guy," Ravi says.

"Yeah, he's really wise," Landon adds as they all follow me to my office.

"I'm sure he is. We're…co-faculty." I turn and get

a good look at them. "He's also my *professor*. I'm taking a class with him." I hope my tone conveys everything I can't say.

The boys look at each other and I can almost see the cogs turning in their head as they realize the implications.

"So you can't...*oh*," Ravi says.

"Ooh, a forbidden romance, I love it!" Omar says, still grinning madly. "Just like in every soap opera and musical I've ever seen!"

Now it's my turn to roll my eyes. "You all can go back to studying now or whatever."

They're still not leaving. "Look, Logan, we only want you to be happy." Ravi sounds so sincere.

"You have our support," Landon says, and Omar nods.

"If you want to support me, then you'll please not say anything to anyone." I fiddle with papers that don't need to be moved. "Just by implying what...you're implying is *dangerous*." I stare intently at Ravi. "Wei is my professor, and he could lose his job."

The boys seem to understand as their faces turn serious.

"You know, I'm dating my TA," Landon says. "He had to fill out this form that says there's going to be no conflict of interest. It's on the school website."

My pulse is still going a mile a minute. "He's not my TA, though." I rapidly tap my fingers on my desk. "Wei and I are...just *friends*. And co-faculty. And student and teacher." I'm looking down, still a nervous wreck. Am I *this* transparent? If these kids can see it, then Wei probably can, too.

"Got it. Our lips are sealed, man." Ravi nods and Landon

stares at him in agreement.

"We got your back," Omar adds. "We won't say a word."

"There's nothing to say." I finally look back up at them. "But thank you."

They smile and leave me in peace. Once they're gone, the silence in the Athletics Center is deafening. I'm so used to spending most of my time here, I'd forgotten what having friends and a life was like.

I wonder what Wei and his family are doing right now. For a brief moment, I'm tempted to call him to ask them all to dinner, but I stop myself. He has a family, and I have an empty house to return to. I can't act like I'm a part of their home, no matter how badly I want to be.

19: Wei

"You're staring pretty hard there, Brother." I'm startled by Pei's sudden appearance next to me in the living room. It's been over a week since Galen's private soccer lesson, and Logan is back at our place to show him how to throw a softball. He's letting Galen borrow a college men's baseball glove, and it looks hilariously huge on my nephew.

"Well, I'm just..." I wipe my hands on my thighs. "Making sure Galen doesn't get hurt." My throat is dry from lying, and my sister smirks at me.

"Sure." She turns to look out the window with me, sipping her coffee. "Logan is pretty hot."

"What?" I yelp.

"Come on." She laughs. "It's OK to admit it."

"I don't...um..." I look back out the window. Logan gives Galen a high five, and they break out in laughter. "He's...still my student," I mutter.

"Uh-huh." She takes another long sip. "For how long?"

"I never actually..."

"For. How. Long?" she repeats. I can hear the smirk in her voice.

I let out a deep exhale. "Twenty-four days. Twenty until I submit my grades and he technically has no influence on me, the teacher." I hang my head, embarrassed.

Pei laughs. "It's fine. No need to be ashamed. It's just us. I won't tell."

"Nothing to tell." I look back up at her. "We haven't...*done* anything."

"Didn't you guys, like, hook up a few weeks ago? When he first had breakfast with us?"

"No! We just..." I shrug my shoulders and wipe my hands again. "He...wasn't feeling well, so I let him stay over."

"So no sex then?"

"Sister, ew, please, I don't want to talk about this!"

She giggles and sits me down on the couch so we're turned away from the window. "Brother, it's OK. Why do you think I let you take a basement room with a door that locks?"

"Because all human adults deserve privacy?"

"Exactly. Privacy to..." She looks around, trying to find the words. "To date. By my accounts you've never had a serious relationship."

"Neither have you," I reply, annoyed.

"I had *one*, it bombed, and now I have a son." She touches my shoulder. "Wei, you're a great father figure for Galen, but you deserve to have a life. To go out and be young. To fall in love, maybe?"

My eyebrows jump and I feel my throat get dry. Before I can even cough, the front door opens.

"Mommy, Logan taught me all sorts of stuff and I'm gonna be the next Jeter!"

We both chuckle. "Of course, dear. What do you say to Logan?"

"Thanks, Logan!"

"No problem, little man. Why don't you go get washed up for lunch?"

Galen nods and dashes away. Hearing Logan be responsible with Galen makes a sparkler go off in my heart. Shit, this man keeps getting sexier.

"Thanks for today," Pei says.

"No problem, I had fun. Plus, it keeps me active."

"Hey, so Friday is Wei's birthday." My eyebrows jump again. I completely forgot, what with juggling jobs and father figure duty. We don't usually celebrate at all, considering we have no other family.

"Oh?"

"Yeah. Do you want to go out to dinner with us?"

"You don't have to," I say, even though I'm not sure why.

"I'd love to!" Logan beams at me.

"Perfect! Badger my brother for the details so he won't forget, OK?"

Logan chuckles. "For sure. Have a good afternoon, you two."

After he leaves, we watch him walk down the path to his car through the window.

"He's got a nice ass too," Pei mutters.

"Sister!" I hiss, then pick up a pillow and hit her with it.

20: Logan

It's Tuesday afternoon, and I'm in my office trying to find the perfect gift for Wei online. I hear a knock on my open door and come face-to-beautiful-face with him.

"Hey." His simple smile is enough to light up a night sky.

"Hey yourself, Assistant Professor Wong." I offer my most flirtatious grin while I close my PC. "What brings you here?"

"Are you going to this Spring Fair thing on Sunday?"

"Yeah, of course!" The annual Spring Fair takes place on the quad. The student groups set up booths for charity, and there are lots of games and food. It's overall a fun event. "It's your first time?"

"Yeah, but QPU is going to be there, so I have to help man the booth."

"I guess I'll see you there. The student athletes are always holding some wacky charity activity, and it's fun to play along."

"Nice." Wei chuckles. "Good to know I'll be among friends there."

"Of course." I study his face for a moment. "Is that all you came to see me for?"

"Oh right. I also wanted to let you know I finally decided what I want to do for my birthday this Saturday."

"Shoot."

"I'd like to go to The Player One bar. Their wings are divine."

"Oh, sweet," I reply.

"Yeah, and Galen can play some games. He'll be so overstimulated he'll pass out when he gets home."

We both chuckle. "Sounds like a plan." I nod and lower my voice. "Is there a reason you couldn't text me that? I still have a few hours here, so it's not like I can drive you home."

Wei's cheeks redden and he looks left and right. "I, uh, wanted coffee? The coffee bar here is... exceptional."

I grin. "Sure, Wei. Whatever you say."

He smiles back at me, and I feel a silent spark pass between us.

"If it isn't Wei Wong!" The shrill sound of Aggie's voice cuts through our moment, and she appears in my doorway, her hand immediately on Wei's shoulder.

Wei's back stiffens. "Aggie," he says in a serious tone.

"Professor Hark." I nod at her.

"I came here to visit Logan, but I got you too? Talk about a two-for-one handsome man special!" She laughs at her weird joke, and we both plaster on fake smiles.

"Right, well, I have to go practice." Wei nods. "I'll talk to you...*both*, later."

"Bye honey!" Aggie waves him off, then walks in and sits on my desk. She towers above me while I sit in my chair and I look at her calmly.

"Do you need something?"

"Oh definitely. I came here for my weekly dose of wondering what you were doing this weekend?" She grins and I raise one eyebrow.

"I'm...busy." I look away, hoping she'll finally take a hint.

"Oh Logan, you've been acting awfully strange lately. You're all happy and cheerful." She crosses her legs and looks up at the ceiling like she's thinking.

"I'm always in a good mood."

"But those smiles were always so fake. I know a thing or two about acting. Speaking of which, this semester's theater production is killing me. Mark my words, I am *nabbing* an assistant next semester." She shakes her head and throws a serious expression my way. "Logan, despite all my big talk, I'm not actually a gossip. I would never talk about your personal life with anyone if it upset you, and I'm so glad you found someone who makes you really smile. I swear, I do want you to be happy."

I'm touched by her sincerity. For as loud of a personality she is, Aggie has always been helpful to me at work. I feel like we really are friends and that I can trust her. "Thanks Profes...I mean, Aggie."

We smile at each other for a moment "This person you're dating must be really special," she says.

"Well I'm still not...technically dating anyone."

"You said 'technically.' That means there *is* someone."

"Would you please keep your voice down?"

Feeling the emergence of gossip, Aggie leans her head in. "OK, so what's going on?"

I debate telling her the truth. I do trust her as a friend, and honestly, this secret crush has been eating me up inside for weeks, so I need to tell someone. "Look." I lower my voice and glance at the doorway to make sure no one's around. "If I tell you, you have to swear to not tell anyone."

She puts her hands together, like she's praying. "Not a soul, I promise, so *spill*: who are you dating?"

"I'm not dating anyone. But...I think Wei Wong and I like each other."

Aggie's eyes light up and her mouth opens in a half-grin. She gets up from the desk and grins. "Honestly, that's kind of a turn-on."

"Uh...sure. But you can't tell anyone 'cause we both could get in trouble."

"Why? We're faculty."

"He's my professor," I hiss. "And we haven't officially made any moves yet." I rub my temple. "And frankly, I'm still not even sure how much he likes me."

"You know what you should do? Take a walk with him under the stars. I guarantee the power of the romantic night sky will get him to fall for you. That's just cosmic science." I lead her out.

"I don't think that's a thing, but thanks, I'll keep it in mind." Before I close the door, I take a good look at her. "Why are you being so cool about this?"

"Look, Logie. I know I come on strong sometimes, but I, like I said, I want you to be happy. You're a great guy, and you deserve someone who brings light and joy into your life. Plus, I'm a huge rom-com addict, so I'd love to see your happily ever after. Watching two gorgeous men like yourselves fall in love and do the nasty? Talk about a girl's fantasy!"

I chuckle and shake my head. "Well, thanks again. Hey, his birthday is coming up, and I have no idea what to get him. Any advice?"

"Consider his likes and hobbies and whatnot." She shrugs, and my eyebrows furrow.

"Why did I not think of that before?"

"When it comes to grand romantic gestures, I'm a genius." She spins her heels and walks away cackling.

It makes me glad to know I have a friend in Aggie. Once the coast is clear, I pull out my phone and make a call to someone I haven't thought of in a while. "Hey Otis, it's Logan."

21: Wei

I'm actually looking forward to my birthday this year, which is an exciting change of pace. Usually it comes and goes and we don't do anything special. My aunt used to buy me some stuff I wanted before she abandoned us, and now my sister gets me something nice, but otherwise, it's simply another day of the year.

Today, though, seeing Logan's glowing face walking into The Player One bar is enough of a present to make my whole day special. "Hey, happy birthday, man!" He gives me a big hug, then pulls away all too soon. Damn, his cologne smells good; the woodsy scent combined with his tight black button-down makes me dizzy with arousal.

"Thanks," I reply, feeling flustered. "The big three-oh."

"Yup."

"Loganloganlogan!" Galen hops up and down next to me in the booth. "I'm gonna go play some arcade games!"

"Oh, awesome!" He laughs.

"We're going to order food first," Pei says.

Galen pouts, but Logan looks at him and says "Hey, I *am* pretty hungry." He rubs his stomach for emphasis, and I can't help but giggle. This gorgeous man fits right in with my family, and an emotion I don't recognize flickers across my chest.

After we order, Logan and I take Galen to play an arcade game about fighting robots. After one game, I sit back down next to my sister. "Do you want to play something?"

"No, as long as you boys are having fun, I'm happy. Besides I did three twelve-hour shifts in a row, so sitting down feels like paradise." We exchange rueful smiles; being a licensed practical nurse and a single mom is no easy feat, even with me taking on as much responsibility as I do helping to raise Galen.

Pei and I gaze over at Logan and my nephew, who are playing at a pinball machine themed around cartoon UFOs. "He's so good with him," she points out.

"Yeah, he is." My whole body gets warm at the sight of this sexy man being the fun uncle for Galen I never could be.

"It's like I can hear you swooning from here." I whip my head around and Pei chuckles.

"Huh...what..." I stammer, my face feeling warm. Thank goodness I'm saved from further embarrassment by the waiter bringing our food. Once the plates are settled, Galen and Logan return, grinning.

"Uncle Wei, Logan told me all about the *real* stars. He said he goes camping sometimes and looks at the twinkling little stars, and it's not too far! Can we go with him one day?"

"Uhh..." I turn to Pei and then look at Logan. "We've never done that. We don't even have tents."

"I have an extra tent." Logan shrugs. "I mentioned to little man over here how on a clear night, you can see constellations at a campsite in Breen Park. I went there as a kid with my parents. It blew me away." He pours ketchup on his plate. "I'd love to take you all."

I frown slightly. I'm really not much of an outdoorsman.

"I'm off next weekend. We can celebrate your end of the semester," Pei says. I turn to my sister and glare at her. She's trying to hide her grin while she eats a chicken wing.

"Please, Uncle Wei," Galen whines and uses the baby eyes that tend to get him his way. Now I know I'm out numbered.

"If you finish your coleslaw, then sure." He cheers, and Logan giggles at him.

"Oh, by the way, I have a gift for you, but it's at my house. It's not done yet, but I wanted to show it to you. Do you wanna come over?"

"Well I don't think—"

"Go after dinner," Pei says, interrupting me. She slices up some chicken for Galen, then continues. "Logan can drive you home, right?"

"You're really not far." Logan grins, eating a french fry. "Neighbors, remember?"

His flirtatious tone almost has me chuckling. "I do like presents."

We spend the next hour eating and playing games. Pei and Galen cheer when I beat Logan at the robot fighting game. The three of us haven't laughed that hard in a long time, possibly ever. It's the best birthday I can remember.

{

"It won't take that long I promise. Then I'll drive you home." We're at Logan's house, which is a huge, secluded, white structure in the neighborhood on the other side of Dugan's Brook. On a good day, I could probably walk here since it's so close.

"Is that what you say on dates?"

He whips his head around, face now pink. My serious face shatters into a laugh and soon he cracks up as well.

"Very funny. Follow me." He leads me through the house to another doorway that opens to what looks like the garage. He turns on the lights, and the garage appears to be Logan's woodworking shop.

"Ta-da!" Logan points to the table in the middle. On it lies a three-feet by two-feet curved wooden arc structure with holes in it. Upon closer inspection, there are metal prongs with two strings in the middle area. *No way.*

"Is this a—"

"Um, so it still needs a lot of work. And I still need to sand it and fix some bolts. I'm ordering the strings online. Woodworking is a bit of a hobby of mine, but I'm really rusty. The person I got it from said the bones are still good, and it seems sturdy, and it can only hold twenty strings. Hopefully that'll be enough to um, function properly for you but...happy birthday?"

My ears are still buzzing in shock. No one's ever done anything like this for me.

"You made me a harp?" I look up at him and see him blushing and shrugging, as if unsure that I like it.

"You said you've always wanted to play it. And you never had any room, but this one's portable. This way, you can work on it at home. At least that's what the guy I got the frame from claimed." I stare at his face for a moment while he looks down at the instrument—my gift. He's so fucking handsome and everyday I'm floored by his generosity.

He turns to me, still unsure. "Is it...is that cool? I still have to sand some parts down and—"

I don't even realize I'm doing it; it's like an instinct. I lean in like the first night we met when I kissed his cheek. My mouth is on his before I can even think to stop it.

His lips on mine feel like a downpour. It's like the dam that held back my feelings for him for months has been cracking, and the idea of him making me an instrument broke that wall. Everything I have, everything I am, and everything I want, is in this kiss.

Logan and I just fit together, in every way, like some grand design had us destined to crash into each other.

His lips part as he brings his head down, and soon enough, our tongues meet. Tasting the inside of Logan's mouth is intoxicating. If his moan is any indication, he's loving this too. He cradles my back in his arms, and his towering body pushes up against mine. I feel his hardness against my front and it delights me, so I push forward as well. Before I can do more, however, common sense hits me like a boomerang.

He's still my student.

Shit. I'm kissing my student.

Fuck.

I pull away, horrified. Not good, not good at all, Wei. This is wrong.

"Hey, what..." Logan's eyes look dazed, like he just woke up from a twelve-hour nap. "What's wrong?"

"I'm sorry. I shouldn't have. That was completely inappropriate."

"It's OK." He puts his hands on my shoulders. "I wanted you to do it. Just like at Christmas." He chuckles but I'm still freaking out.

"I shouldn't have...I'm a professor now and..."

"I swear I won't tell." His voice is husky, filled with desire. He leans in again, but before he can kiss me, I push his arms off.

"No, no. You're my student. I have to go." I walk briskly past him through the hall and out the door. I'm shaking my head as I hear him shout after me.

Fortunately, the early spring night is not too cold, so I run. My heart is beating rapidly, but I don't care. It takes me thirty minutes to get home. I'm huffing and sweating by the time I'm at the front door, and I lean on a wall.

I don't want to see my family right now, and I don't dare check my phone.

Shit, I could have ruined my teaching career, all for a kiss, all because I couldn't keep my feelings at bay for another few fucking weeks.

I put my finger on my lips—I can still taste him. That's the worst part of all of this: I liked it, and I want to do it again.

22: Logan

Sunday morning is a busy one on campus as student groups roam around to set up for the Spring Fair. I do my part early to hand out gear to the athletes who are participating; the athletics department raises a lot of money running contests for charity. Once I'm done, I lock up and make my way to the quad to get my mind off things.

Once there, I see the soccer boys standing next to what appears to be—heaven help us all—a dunk tank. Before I can complain, I see the man of my dreams sitting across from them, several yards away, at a separate booth. I'm relieved to know Wei is alright, but nervous about being so close to him.

The kiss we shared last night was nothing short of amazing. It's been a while for me, but it's likely the best kiss I've ever had. It felt *so right* to finally have Wei in my arms.

If he asks me to apologize, I might, but if he asks me if I regret it, I'll tell him I don't.

He ran away so quickly I didn't get a chance to talk him down. He looked so horrified, panicking, but I was so dazed I let him take off. I understand his job could be at stake, but he and I are so *so* close to the finish line. Only two more weeks and he won't be my professor anymore.

If he kisses me one more time, though, all bets—and probably my clothes—are coming off.

I sit next to the soccer boys for a bit and make small talk. Soon enough, all their significant others start approaching, as well as a crowd of local families. While they set up the charity dunk tank for Kareem to drop into, I take my leave and walk the few yards to the QPU booth.

Their section has multiple stalls with various games, including a sack-throwing game and a pie-in-the-face station. I sit down next to Wei, and to his credit, he seems perfectly at ease with me.

"Hey, man."

"Wei. How's the booth?"

"It's going well. With all the families milling about, we're hoping to make lots of money for various LGBTQ charities."

"That's awesome." My grin fades, and I steel myself for the awkward conversation. "Listen, about last night—"

"Don't worry about it." Wei waves his hand and smiles.

"But I want to talk about it."

"Please, I'd rather you not." He subtly points around. He's showing me that, while no one's within earshot, there are plenty of students around. "I think it would be best if we didn't talk about it."

"Gotcha." I nod my head, then put a happy face back on. "Well, if you ever want to talk about it...in private, call me."

"I'm..." He looks around again. "I'm busy doing students' grades for the next week. The semester is close to being over."

"Yes?" I furrow my brow, confused. What's he getting at?

"I propose we talk about this *after* I submit your grades.

Once the semester. Is over. Mr. Micucci." His words each carry a heavy emphasis but I think I get what he's saying: he's as ready as I am to make a move once I'm no longer his student.

I grin. "Got it. I'll talk to you later, Assistant Professor Wong."

I get up and walk back over to the athletes. A small crowd has gathered and everyone is laughing now that Kareem has fallen into the dunk tank. There's a lot of activity with people lining up for their chance to throw baseballs, but I only have eyes for the man in the booth across from me.

An hour later, the crowd has grown since staff members started to participate. Coach Dacks is walking out of the dunk tank, his black t-shirt soaked and stuck to his body. He's scowling, but his wife and everyone else is in stitches.

"It's for charity, Coach!" I yell while clapping.

"Yeah, yeah." He takes a towel from his wife. "If it's so important for a good cause, then *you* get in the tank next."

I giggle, ready to say no, when I hear a familiar voice behind me say, "I'd pay twenty bucks for the chance to dunk Mr. Micucci."

Turning around, I see Wei with a smug look on his face. Pretty soon, all the athletes are hollering and Omar is pulling me toward the tank. Everyone's laughing, and some people are chanting "*do it*," but I only have eyes for Wei.

I shrug and hand my phone and belongings to Ravi, knowing he'll keep them safe. I get on the tank seat and shrug at the audience. Kareem hands Wei three softballs and he looks so cocky...It's kind of hot.

"Thanks for the charity money, Wong!" I jeer at him. "Too

bad you don't have the arm to knock me down!" People holler with "*ooh's*" and laugh, but Wei just smirks at me.

"You're right. I don't. But he does." Landon walks up to him, grinning, and Wei hands him the softballs.

My face drops. "Hey now, you can't—"

"I owe Wei a favor!" he yells. He pulls back his arm, and the next thing I know, I'm submerged in water.

When I come up for air, the audience is roaring and Wei is leaning on the tank waiting for me, mouth curled up like the Cheshire cat. "I call shenanigans," I mutter.

"All's fair for charity." He's cute when he's teasing me. I shake my hair out furiously just to get him wet. "Hey!" He laughs.

"All's fair for charity, huh?" I quirk an eyebrow then turn to walk out of the tank.

Soaking wet still, I saunter over to the QPU booth. The student running it is holding Landon's biceps and the two of them look like they're going to jump each other's bones right here. But not before I do what I need to.

"Hey you, I need to do some charity revenge."

"That was *not* my idea!" Landon says. "Not my money either. That was all Wei." Landon points at the man who is now standing to my left, having followed me.

"I know. I'm not here to get revenge on you, Landee." I grin at Wei and he looks horrified.

"What are you doing?" Wei asks.

"I'll donate fifty bucks to pie Assistant Professor Wong in the face."

"Wow!" Landon's boyfriend says. "Fifty bucks? You heard the man, Wei."

"Oh Dane, I'm really not—" Before he can finish, Landon and this guy Dane are pulling him over to the booth. More patrons are now gathering around on this side, laughing. Perfect.

A moment later, Wei's head pops up through the cardboard partition that has a hole cut out of it. Dane hands me an aluminum pie tray filled with whipped cream, and I give him my cash. Wei looks both nervous and amused as I hold up the pie.

"All's fair for charity, right?" I shout, pulling my arm back, ready to throw. At this, the whole crowd roars, but I only have eyes for him, as usual.

I toss the tray and it hits his face with such a satisfactory splat that I'm laughing, along with everyone around me. People cheer and Wei walks backward, removing whipped cream from his eyes. When I go back to join him, he simply shakes his head. He seems to be holding back a laugh while I'm wiping away my tears.

"How does it taste?"

"Delicious." He licks cream off his lips, and I have a momentary urge to lick it all off him. I lead him down the path once I see another professor getting into the pie-throwing booth. The crowd cheers as they get ready for this next charity victim, so no one seems to notice us.

"You look ridiculous." My cheeks still hurt from laughing and he's scowling at me. "See, now we're even."

"I'm covered in dessert. You're all wet, and you look..." He waves his hand at me, but doesn't finish his sentence. *I really want to know what he was going to say.*

"We can get cleaned up back at the Center." We take the five-minute walk down the path to the large silver complex. Because of the Spring Fair, I closed up early, and there are no students around.

"I can get you towels and stuff here." Wei follows me

down to the men's locker room. Upon entering, I realize how alone the two of us are in my building. It's so quiet I can hear the squeaks of our shoes echoing down the hall.

As if reading my mind, Wei turns to me and asks, "Are we really alone here?"

I swallow. "Yeah." I yearn to kiss him, but I don't want to scare him away like last night.

"You got cream all over me." His voice is deep and commanding, and he's maintaining this confident eye contact. Even drenched in whipped cream, he is so sexy. "I'm taking a shower." Before I can object, he whips off his shirt in front of me—fuck.

His body, while not as muscular as mine, is toned in all the right places. It's hairless and smooth and so incredibly *Wei* I can feel my cock immediately perk up in interest. Wei's staring right at me, eyes filled with challenge and longing. *Is he asking me to join him?* Fuck, I haven't breathed in thirty seconds.

"Get me a towel?" He pops the button of his jeans and unzips. I see traces of his pubes as he pushes his pants down and I spin around so fast my neck hurts.

"Uh...OK!" I holler.

"Thanks, Mr. Micucci." I can hear the smirk on his face. He knows he has me flustered. Was this his plan all along?

I walk out of the locker room and close my eyes. I take a deep breath and try to will my erection to go down. Shit, if he asked me to join him in the shower, I'd do it.

I'm not sure what game Wei is playing, but whatever it is, I'm willing to go a few more rounds.

23: Wei

I wash off the remnants of whipped cream in the locker room shower. There are partitions and shower curtains, but I purposefully leave mine open. I stroke myself a bit to fluff my dick for when the man of my dreams sees me naked. Once I hear Logan walk back in, I turn around and really get under the water. I want Logan to watch me, to remember this forever. While we can't kiss, I still want him to want me, and this is the only way I know how. This is my way of telling him to wait for me until the end of the semester.

After a beat, I turn around to see him looking at the ceiling, gripping two towels like his life depends on it.

"Hey man!" I say. He doesn't respond. "Hey, Logan, can you hear me?"

"Uh, yeah." He makes the briefest eye contact then looks down at the floor. He looks so shaken. I almost feel bad for teasing him like this. "I got you that towel."

"What was that?" I heard him. I just want him to look at me.

"I got you that towel!" I shut off the shower and

he finally looks at me.

"Thanks, man." He bites his lip and puts the towel on a bench. *Oh no you don't.* "Hey, I wanted to talk to you about music class."

"Um, yeah?" He's back to staring at the ceiling, now biting his lip.

"Are you ready for your recital tomorrow?"

"Uh...uh yeah. I f-f-feel comfortable." Still wet, I saunter over to him.

"So what are you performing?"

"Bizet's 'Habañera.'" Up close, I notice how red his face is as he continues to avoid my eyes, even as I'm a foot in front of him. Of course, me being rock hard might have something to do with it.

"Ah, from *Carmen*. Great choice." I lean over and pick up the towel. "All about how love...is truly rebellious. Like a bird that won't stay in a cage." I rub my hair with the towel. "Wouldn't you agree, Mr. Micucci?"

"Mhm," he whimpers, eyes still glued upward. Poor guy probably hasn't taken a full breath since I started showering.

Who knew I was such an exhibitionist?

I walk over to my clothes and put on my red boxer briefs. Once I'm done, I turn around to see him already staring at my ass. I'm smirking, but once I catch his eyes, they dart upward again.

I scoff and put on my jeans. "Well, thanks for the shower."

"Anytime. Anything for...co-faculty," he says to the ceiling.

"In a matter of days, that's all we'll be." He looks at me, and I continue. "We won't be student and professor anymore."

"Very true."

I walk up to him, side-to-side, and touch his shoulder. He doesn't move but turns his head. "Maybe we'll see each other on campus this summer, Mr. Micucci." I give him one last flirtatious smirk, then make my exit, hoping Logan is watching me.

The next week goes by in a blur with finalizing grades and the big recital. All of the beginner students do well, much to the approval of Professor Reyes. Logan does a great job with 'Habañera', and when he finishes, I'm probably applauding louder than anyone else. Before he gets off stage, I see him wave at the audience, then at us, the music department. There may have been a private smile only for me, but we've been teasing each other for so long everything he does seems like innuendo. I can't say I mind.

There's still another week left in the semester, but our music class is over, considering we don't do finals. I feel like I'm finally ready to make a move on Logan; no more teasing, no more holding back, and definitely no running away. I want him, and I need him to know it.

That's going to have to wait, however, because today, Logan is driving my whole family north to Breen Park. Once his car pulls up, Galen bolts out the door, and I try my best to follow him. I swear, the kid is more excited to see him than I am.

"Logan, Logan, I've been practicing my spiral throw!"

"Oh really?" He chuckles after going around the car.

"He has," I remark. "He makes me catch it and everything."

"You keep dropping it," Galen says with a pout.

"Hey!" I say with a faux-offense, while Logan laughs.

"You be nice to your uncle," Pei says, coming up from behind me. "His good friend Logan is taking us camping."

"I'm so excited!" Galen says, bobbing up and down.

"Me too. Let me get his car seat." He takes it from my sister and reaches into the back seat of his car while Galen tags along. Once again I'm moved by this sexy man who's constantly looking after my family.

"You looking forward to sleeping under the stars?" my sister asks.

"Uh, yeah." My face gets warm and I try to look at the sky, the pretty pretty sky.

"Uh-huh," she says. "How many days until the end of your semester again?"

"Technically, in a way, it's already over for us." I look at her and notice her stunned expression.

"Ah, so you're really *really* looking forward to this trip." I wince and she sniggers, walking back to the car.

"You ready?" Logan asks once Galen is in his seat.

"I've been ready for quite some time," I mutter to myself.

This trip is going to be legendary.

24: Logan

I've gone camping by myself a few times over the years since my parents died. It's nice to spend some time outdoors. I enjoy taking in the woodsy scent, breathing in the happy memories of coming here as a kid and my folks telling me about the stars.

Today, however, is a much more fun experience with people I've come to care about. I set up the two tents, we walk around the nearby woods, and I point out all the foliage I can recall to Galen. I get the feeling he's never had a goofy uncle figure, what with his actual uncle being his de facto father figure. I can't blame them—I admire him and Pei so damn much for the way they're raising him—but I can tell the kid needs a fun uncle to look up to. The way he latches on to me every time we play sports makes me feel valued in a way I never have before. I've grown quite fond of him.

Not as fond as I am of his uncle, of course. Wei and I keep stealing glances as the four of us walk through the woods. All I can picture is his naked body showering in front of me, teasing me. Fuck, I want him so much.

"You know," Wei says once Galen and Pei are in

the campsite washroom. "I already handed in the grades for the semester. And we don't have music class together anymore."

"I'm very aware of that, Assistant Professor Wong." The mere idea of what he's alluding to has my cock taking interest already, and the sun has barely set. I haven't even started my nefarious plan of seduction yet!

"Not your professor anymore." His voice is deep and husky, and he makes a show of looking me up and down. "We're just...co-faculty."

Fuck, that word is going to give me a boner for the rest of my life now, isn't it?

"I suppose we are, Wei." I grin at him, gazing into his warm eyes.

Before either of us can say more, Pei and Galen return from washing up.

"Are we gonna make s'mores tonight? I read about them online." Galen turns from me to Wei. "Do you know what s'mores are Uncle Wei? It's when you take a graham cracker and chocolate and eat them in the woods!"

"Sure," Wei chuckles. "But you have to eat dinner first."

"Come on, little man. Let's grill up some food for your mom and uncle." I take Galen by the hand and walk him over to our campfire site.

Dinner outside is delicious, and Galen has a great time teaching his mom how to make s'mores. They both entertain the kid by trying to learn his way step-by-step, even though his keep falling over. I tell them all about the stars and constellations and regale Galen with tales about Greek deities flying across the sky. Once it's past nine, I clean up and Pei helps Galen wash up again and go to bed.

Galen is so tired that he doesn't put up a fight to sleep. While we hadn't talked about sleeping arrangements, Pei asks if Wei and I have enough room in our tent, casually letting us know she assumes he and I are going to sleep together.

"I could stay with you two," Wei says, and a flame of disappointment bounces through my chest.

"No way, there's no room," she replies in a hushed voice. "I'm going to relax in the tent. I'm beat from all that walking." She looks between the two of us once I put out the campfire. "It's still early though. You two can hang out."

"I was thinking about taking a night walk," I blurt out quickly, and they both turn at me. "Look at the stars. I brought an extra blanket. Wei, would you...like to come with me?"

"Sure." He turns to his sister.

"Like I said, I'm beat. Plus, I have so many books to read on my phone. I need to make a dent in my 'to-be-read' list. You two go enjoy!" It's dark, but I swear I see her wink at her brother. It's good to know I have the blessing of the two people most important to Wei. Now I need to put my plan into action. I pick up my sitting blanket after Pei closes her tent and begin the trek, Wei not too far behind me.

"I'm pretty sure those four make up the body of Hercules, the constellation."

"A hero made of stars?"

"Yup," I reply. We're both lying on our backs, shoulders touching, staring at the sky. It's a brilliant, clear night, not too cold. Everything about this feels surreal—the stars, this night, and this amazing man whose family has begun to mean so much to me.

We planted this comfy blanket about a ten-minute walk away. It's early May, so barely anyone has come to the park, and we've had the whole place to ourselves all day. Now, it's just Wei and me. Only the trees and the cosmos are watching us lie here, the sounds of bugs chirping adding to the ambience.

Aggie was right; the night sky filled with stars really is something. I'm hoping it's as romantic for Wei as it is for me. I turn my head and notice he is already staring at me. The clarity of the Moon reflects on his perfect face, and I want to kiss him so badly. But no, I need him to cross that line. He's done it before, but I want him to do it again, but this time, with no regrets.

"Wei."

"Yeah?"

"You have to know how I feel about you by now, right?" My voice is low, pleading. I'm not even breathing as I wait for his response.

He sits upright, and I do the same. *Shit, is he going to run away again?*

"I...I'm not sure."

"Well, let me make it crystal clear." I look up at the stars and hope the celestial bodies will give me the courage to say what I need to next. "I...want to be with you.

Romantically. I like you a lot."

"Why?" I look over to see him looking down. "Why me? No one's ever wanted to be with me for more than like, a night or two. I keep pushing you away, and yet I can't seem to shake you. Not that I tried all that hard."

That last part brings a curve to my lips. "Because I'm into...everything about you. You're talented... gorgeous. You care so much about your nephew and sister. You calm me down for the first time in *years*. Like harmonies, two music notes spaced apart that fit together. When you're around...it's like harmony."

Wei is silent, and I feel like I've messed everything up.

"You're like harmony to me too." His voice is barely audible, but I'm going to remember his lips saying that for the rest of my life.

Maybe it's the blessing of the stars, but when I lean in to place my mouth on his, he puts his hand on my cheek and kisses me back.

25: Wei

I lean in and kiss this beautiful, amazing man, the same one who just confessed his feelings for me. I breathe in his scent, the same one I've been trying to memorize; only this time, there's no panic. I forget about everything else in the world except the stars and the trees around us. I refuse to hold back any longer. He's essentially not my student anymore, so I can finally kiss him the way I want to.

And boy, do I want to. Logan Micucci knows how to kiss. His lips are warm and soft, and when his tongue touches mine again, the blood in my head flows downward. I caress his perfect stubble with my right hand while I moan into his mouth.

Pulling back for a moment, I can see he's smiling. His eyes are filled with hunger as they reflect the cosmos above. "I've wanted that for a while."

"Well, I want more." *Did I just growl?*

I pull him in and kiss him again, this time more frantically. I shift my body so that I'm lying flat again, and Logan is along for the ride. He hoists his legs so that now he's straddling me, knees on the blanket, almost like he's trapping me—more like the other way around.

He leans down, and I catch my lips on his delicious neck. Hearing him moan, knowing that I'm doing it for him, gets me rock-hard instantly. Fuck, this guy is so sexy, and I've wanted him for so long. We've been playing this edging game since day one, and it's time to get what I want, what we both need.

He pulls back and studies me, the stars above him like a halo. "Is this alright?" He adjusts the bulge in his pants. "I don't want to like...take advantage of you."

"Green light, Logan." I undo the top button and unzip my jeans. "You've wanted me for a long time, haven't you?"

"Yes," he whispers. His eyes are blown wide as he looks down at the hardness in my boxers.

"Well, I'm not your professor anymore." I graze his erection with my hand, and that seems to set him off. He leans back in and starts to suck on my neck, and I moan— mission accomplished.

"Mm...you're so sexy," he mutters against the skin.

"No, you are." My eyes are rolling back. It's been way too long, and I might come soon without him even touching my cock. I grab his firm ass with my left hand, and with my right I try to undo his button and zipper. He takes mercy on me by lifting up and undoing it himself.

"What do you want to...?" He huffs, a heated question, as he pulls his pants slightly lower. The spring of his hard cock releasing makes me drool, and, on instinct, I reach out to stroke it.

"Uhh," he groans, bending back down. He reaches into my boxers and pulls out my leaking dick. Now, with his face in my neck, our erections are perfectly aligned.

My eyes are screwed shut as he begins to thrust. I can't tell if the stars I'm seeing are from the delicious strokes he's giving me or if it's the night sky. Either way, I could do this forever, with this sexy Facilities Manager bringing me to that glorious climax.

Forever is apparently only a minute or so because all too soon, Logan is whimpering in my ear.

"I'm so close...Wei, I'm about to..."

"Yes," I hiss in reply. "I'm gonna come, Logan. You want to come with me?" Another delicious moan into my neck is the only response. He strokes me faster, and I match his pace. There's so much leakage and I feel his leg muscles quivering as I grip his ass over me.

I pull his head up, then catch his lips again, and I feel one last guttural moan vibrate against my mouth. He's coming all over me, and his hand jerks me quickly until I'm returning fire a few seconds later.

After we're both satisfied, he rolls over, gasping for air. My legs finally stop quivering, and we lie there for two whole minutes, trying to catch our breaths. I don't even look at him, unsure if he's staring at the constellations like me.

Pretty soon, the awkwardness sets in. Did I do too much, cross a line? Did I not do enough?

"I'm sorry if I...finished too soon," he whispers. I look over to see him staring at the sky. "I swear, I can last longer." He chuckles. "You're just so hot. Next time, I promise I'll do more for you."

"Next time?" He turns to me, those gorgeous brown eyes twinkling in the stars.

"Ye...yeah," he says. "This isn't a one-and-done,

Wei. I meant it. I've never...been like...I...I meant it." He's looking up and stammering. I link my left hand in his right.

"I like you too, Logan." We stay there for a little while longer, letting the heavenly bodies of light embrace us.

"I'm sure they're still sleeping." The sun is shining through the tent, and I hear my sister whispering. "Let's wait for them."

"But we were gonna go hiking!" I hear my nephew whining, and I know it's time for us to get up.

I stretch, then notice that I'm wrapped around Logan. Happy memories of last night return to me. We confessed our feelings, kissed, then shared the best orgasm I've ever had, all under the night sky. We'd used the blanket to wipe off the mess on our crotches and walked back to the campsite. Here, without even asking, I curled into his large sleeping bag and had the best sleep in years, spooning this man.

Logan rolls over and yawns. His doe-eyed morning eyes shine when he looks at me and smiles. "Morning," he murmurs.

"Morning, you."

He studies me for a moment, then his eyebrows furrow in concern. "Are we cool? About last night, was it... Do you...?"

I put my hand on his chin and curl closer to him.

"I don't regret last night." My mouth is so close to his, but morning breath be damned, he needs to know this, now. "If that's what you're asking." I give him a peck him on the lips, and pinkness spreads across his face. "But we should probably keep it under wraps for the next two weeks."

"I can do that." He grins, and I swear, I'll never be more attracted to another human than I am to him right now.

"I think they're awake, Mommy!" We hear my nephew whisper in a tone so loud it would have woken us up anyway. We both quietly giggle and get up.

We spend the day hiking and cleaning up our campsite, and then it's finally time for the four of us to drive home. I'm going to miss Breen Park and the magic it brought to me and my crush. It takes a lot to keep our hands off each other all day and at the burger place where we have dinner when we get back. Logan keeps throwing me looks like he's a starving man and I'm his favorite meal. My sister keeps giving us knowing glances as well, which makes my cheeks warm and forces me to look back down.

It's getting dark by the time Logan is unloading his car.

"What do you say to Logan?" Pei asks my nephew.

"Thank you, Logan!"

"OK, let's get going so you can take a bath." She throws us both a look. "I'll see you inside in a bit, Brother." Her tone is clearly saying that I should take my time saying goodnight. Lord knows what I want to do with him can't happen out here in the open.

Once she's gone, I twiddle my thumbs and look over at Logan to see him already staring at me, a curve on his lips.

"I had a really good time this weekend." His voice is deep and sexy, like he wants to say so much more.

"Me too." We look at each other in silence before we both awkwardly chuckle. "I, um, should get going."

"Alright."

I turn to walk away before he tugs at my wrist and spins me around. He's looking at me intently, inches away from my face. "Wei, would you like to..." He glances down and bites his lip. "I still have your gift. Next weekend, do you want to come pick it up?"

I grin, my cheeks feeling warm. "My sister will be home, so I could come over."

"I can cook dinner!" he blurts. "To celebrate the, um, end of the semester."

"And the class where I teach you will be officially over."

"Exactly."

"That sounds nice. Dinner at your place. It's a date."

He grins, then walks away. Before he can get in the car, something compels me to go around and stop him. I push him against the door, grab his collar, then pull his lips onto mine. He tastes so good, and when his tongue enters my mouth, I can't help but moan.

I didn't get to make out as a teenager, and I've never kissed anyone as sexy as Logan, so I'm making up for lost time.

Once I finally pull off for air, I study the dazed but satiated look on his face. If he's feeling how I'm feeling, he can't get enough of me either. "OK, I'm going inside for real this time. Goodnight Mr. Micucci."

"Goodnight Assistant Professor Wong." He grins, kisses me on the cheek, and finally gets in the car. Walking back to my house, drunk on the taste of Logan, for the first time in my life, I'm more than just satisfied. I'm enchanted, ecstatic, and hopeful. In short, I'm happier than I've been in *really* long time.

26: Logan

I don't get to see Wei all week, but that's for the best. Music class is over, and the grades are being processed —not that I care about my grade, because I'm not trying to get a degree. This is all for the best; if I go to see Wei, it'll lead to some naughty times in the Fine Arts building, and I'm not trying to mess this up. We text a lot, usually flirty messages, and I can't wait for our date on Saturday.

Wei Wong has me looking forward to things for the first time since my parents died. The way he makes me feel is nothing short of a miracle.

I spend all day Saturday cleaning the house. While I never leave the main living areas cluttered, I want it to look extra spotless for when my handsome date arrives. I take a break to go grocery shopping for food, chocolates, wine, lube, and condoms—you know, the essentials.

That evening, I'm boiling pasta when he texts me that he's at the front door, and my heart starts to pound. I haven't been on a first date since I was a teenager, and even then I never took it seriously. Now, here I am, smoothing over my hair in the foyer mirror and sniffing my armpits.

The cologne is still working, and not a hair is out of place. "*Go get 'em stud,*" I whisper to my reflection.

When I open the door, the sight takes my breath away. Wei is wearing a black button-down shirt that hugs him in all the right areas. He's beaming at me and holding a small bouquet of tulips. He looks so good my jaw drops.

"Hey, Logan!" His face falls. "What's wrong?"

"Nothing!" I yelp, trying to shake the hypnosis from my eyes.

He looks down at his shirt. "Do I look OK?"

"You look amazing." That earns me an honest-to-goodness blush when he looks back up.

"Here, these are for you." He hands me the flowers.

"What's the occasion?" I ask with a grin.

"For...the end of the semester?"

"Right." I nod with a smirk. "Come on in." He walks in and I close the door. "Glad the semester is finally over?"

"Yeah. Though I still have to take some classes for my doctorate in the summer semester. Plus, a few students are taking a summer course of mine."

"I know. I signed up for one. I'm your student all over again this summer, Professor."

He stops dead in his tracks, and I turn around. The look of horror on his face is priceless. I can't hold it in for more than a moment and start cracking up.   "I'm kidding!"

He breathes a sigh of relief with his eyes closed and I start howling with laugher. "You ass. I was about to walk out of here!" he says. We're both in stitches as we walk down the foyer.

I lead him to the right where my kitchen is

bustling with dinner prep. "Hope you like pasta. I'm going to fry up some chicken as well."

"That sounds delicious."

I get back to my pot and stir it slightly. "The pasta is almost done. So we should be able—"

I'm interrupted by Wei reaching over and turning off the stovetop. "Good, I'm glad it's almost done."

His voice is deep and his eyes are challenging. His chest is almost brushing my shoulder and somehow the room just got several degrees warmer.

"Uh...what are you—"

"Logan, there are certain...*activities* I don't want to do after dinner. Things that a full stomach would make extremely inconvenient." He gets on his toes and leans into my ear. "Things I want to do to you."

Oh fuck.

I shiver, and he steps back out of my space. "So what do you say? We can have dinner and small talk after, but right now..." He walks his fingers up my sleeved arm. "I'd like to celebrate you and me no longer being professor and student." The heat in his eyes is undeniable. He could probably ask me to give him my car and I'd hand him the keys, that's how gone I am for him.

I give a dumb nod and swallow. "I'm uh...down for that." I reach down and put my hand in his. He raises it and gives it a kiss—goosebumps.

"Bedroom?" he asks, like it's a question.

* * *

Once everything in the kitchen is turned off—dinner can wait, this is a matter of utmost importance—we make it to my darkened room upstairs. Wei makes a show of turning around, undoing the buttons on his shirt, and walking backwards.

"You know, Pei and Galen don't need me home at all tonight." He eyes me up and down, not even bothering to be subtle. "We can take this as slow or as fast as you want." Fuck, if I wasn't horny five seconds ago, I am now.

I blink twice and remember how to speak. "What do... uh...What do you want to do?"

"Well, I can top." He shrugs. Then, without breaking eye contact, he pulls the rest of his shirt off and throws it far, far away. "I've also prepped myself. So what do you say Logan—do you want to be inside me?"

I'm never going to forget this moment for as long as I live.

I nod, mouth open, probably drooling, and move forward. Capturing his sweet lips, I feel him unbutton my shirt. Our kisses turn frantic, and we quickly pick up the pace, taking everything off and ending up in bed.

"Condoms...mm...bedside table," I mutter against his lips, holding him down.

He pulls back and looks up at me, grinning. "You're prepared?"

Two can play that game. I reach down and finger the entrance to his hole. "Not as prepared as you," I growl.

His eyes roll back as he moves his hips up to grant me easier access. "OK, deal," he moans. I scramble over to get the condoms and lube. Then, I move back to the edge of the bed and Wei crawls over.

"Fuck, you are..." I shake my head staring at

him. "So sexy." I roll the condom on and move closer to him.

"So are you. I really want this." He moves closer to me and lifts his ass up. "I need you inside me."

Hell yeah.

I lube him up and position myself. "Let me know if you want me to stop."

"I cleaned myself out before I got here." He turns back to me. "And I've been waiting for you since the day we met." He winks and gets back into position. OK, this is the best day of my life, and I'm not even inside him yet.

Not wanting to stay in my head, I lick one stripe up his lubed, clean hole. He responds with a thick moan and it makes me dizzy with anticipation. I pull back, grab his hips, and line myself up. "I want you so bad." Hunching over, I kiss his spine, hoping he knows I mean every word.

"Show me, baby." *Did he just call me 'baby?'* His words make my heart burst and I can see a beautiful future with him. I want to feel Wei in my bed decades from now. But to start, we have tonight.

I push in, and he groans. "Wei, is that OK?"

"Keep going," he huffs. "Don't stop unless I tell you. But *ohmygod* I need you Logan."

"Fuck yeah, baby. Let me give it all to you." Holding his hips, I thrust even more. I pick up the pace and it feels so damn good. Moments later, he's hard and playing with himself.

Shit, that is *so hot*. After a few minutes of fucking him, his moans become a higher pitched whimper. He's jerking himself, but somehow I know he needs more. No, I need more.

"Wei." I stop and he cranes his neck around. "Let me suck you off?"

He nods and I pull out. He immediately flips over—so limber!—and now this beautiful man is in front of me, hard and aching. I immediately put the head of his dick in my mouth and finger his wet hole.

"Fuck, Logan!" He shouts my name, like I'm the only thing that matters. I'm proud of myself as he howls, shooting in my mouth while I finger him.

Once I'm done swallowing his load, I flop onto the bed, rip off the condom, and start to jerk myself off. Just seeing Wei here, in my room, sweaty and satisfied, is enough to get me there. Before I can, he pushes my hand off and grips my dick. I immediately start thrusting into it like a dog in heat.

Like last week, this orgasm has me seeing stars. I shout in ecstasy and my semen splashes onto his hip. Almost a full minute later, the spasms subside and I push away his hand.

When blood finally returns to my brain, I open my eyes to see Wei already looking at me. His face is flushed, the room reeks of sex, but he's still the most beautiful thing I've ever seen.

"Was that worth the wait, stud?"

To answer him, I lean over and kiss him, hard, as if we'd never kissed before. "Baby, I'd wait a decade if it meant having sex with you again."

We both giggle, still euphoric from the post-orgasm high, and I lay on his chest and breathe. I've spent years wishing I could go back to the past, and this last semester I wanted to fast forward to summer. Now, I just want to be in this moment with Wei.

27: Wei

"There we go." He plates one last piece of chicken on the pasta and a bed of lettuce. "Dinner is served."

We take the plates to the dining room table where a couple of glasses of wine are ready for us. We got cleaned up after our romp in the sheets, but I'm only wearing my pants. "It's kinda hot in here. You sure you need the shirt?" I ask coyly.

Logan grins at me. "I was frying chicken, didn't want burns on my chest. Do you want me to ditch the shirt?"

I pretend to mull it over. "Mmm...Well yes, yes I do, please."

He chuckles and takes it off, and we sit down. Fuck, his torso is the stuff of legends. Seeing him shirtless will never get old.

"Delicious." I pick up my fork. "And I'm sure the food is good, too." I wink at him to make it obvious.

Logan breaks out in his signature brilliant smile. "I thought you wouldn't be as flirty after having sex."

"Who said we're done for tonight?" I mutter. He

nearly spits up his pasta, and I chuckle. He drinks some wine, then clears his throat.

"To new beginnings."

I hold out my cup. "To the start of...something good." We clink glasses and take a sip. We quietly eat for a minute, having worked up an appetite.

"How is it?"

"It's really good, thanks." I look down for a moment, then decide to ask the burning question. "So, we should probably talk about what happens when I leave here."

"Tonight or tomorrow morning?" He raises his eyebrows while looking at me, and my dick starts to take an interest again. What am I, a teenager?

"That depends." I clear my throat. "We never discussed...what we would do once the semester ended. But..." My face gets warm, and I see his eyes are on me, waiting. "I'd like...a relationship with you."

"Like boyfriends? Like, exclusive boyfriends?"

My heart starts to race. "If you want." I shrug, looking away, testing out my poker face.

He puts his hand on mine and says, "I want to be your boyfriend, too."

Fireworks go off in my heart as he smiles at me.

We both go back to eating, and Logan says, "I didn't say that just to get you to spend the night."

"You couldn't kick me out now if you tried."

"Good." I can hear the grin on his face. "Have you dated recently? It's okay if you have."

"Not recently." I stare right at him and continue. "I was kinda fixated on this tall guy I know this semester." He smiles at this. "How about you?"

He shakes his head and chews on some pasta. "I haven't...*wanted* anything since before my parents died."

Of course. "If you need to talk to a therapist about it..."

"I'm fine." He shrugs. "How are you? You don't seem to have as much trauma as me."

"We don't really remember our parents. We don't know what we missed."

"What about your aunt? The one who raised you."

I shrug, eating some pasta. "It's nothing. She's moved on. I'm fine."

"Are you sure? I know some university people who could help me search for her and contact her."

"No, no, please." I aggressively cut into a slab of chicken. "I don't want you to..."

"OK..." His voice is small, and an awkward silence passes between us. "I'm really messing up on this first date conversation-ing, aren't I?"

I chuckle. "It's alright."

"I want to get to know you, is all. All about you. You fascinate me, Wei. Ever since I met you, I..." I look up and wait for him to finish, but he's concentrating on cutting his food. "You bring such light into my life, or something..."

I stop breathing. A burning sensation flashes through my body. No one's ever cared about me this much. Logan looks up, confused. "Was that...was that weird of me to say? I'm sorry I—"

"You light up my life, too." I smile and look back down at my food, trying to contain all the feelings I have for him.

* * *

141

After we clean up—he does the dishes while I wrap up the leftovers and I use the spare toothbrush he gave me—Logan tells me to relax in the living room. I look at the pictures on the wall. There are so many memories. He seemed like such a happy kid. In each family portrait, his mom looks so much like him, but his dad is tall and scruffy. I never had these family photos as a kid. Maybe one day I'll have portraits with someone special as well, someone tall with kind, brown eyes.

"Ta-da!" Logan sings, walking into the room. His hulking body carries a cleaner version of the harp he gifted me two weeks ago.

"Wow, it's gorgeous." I put it on the table and run my hand along the top of it. The dark-brown wood gives it an old-time feel, but with the strings on, you can hardly tell it's been refurbished. I sit down and play each string. Afterward, I turn to see Logan staring at me, eyes moist. "What's wrong?"

"Nothing." His gaze drops to my lips, and he leans in again, kissing me like I'm the last man on Earth. "I... love hearing you play."

I'm sure I'm blushing. "If you think this is good, you should hear me on the piano."

"Alright!" Logan blurts. He walks away, and I put down the harp and follow him. In the next room, I'm left stunned; he has an ornate grand piano and a shelf filled with what look to be dozens of music books.

"Do you..." He puts his hands in his pockets and shrugs. "Do you want to play something?"

"Do you want me to play something?" I'm teasing him but he's still not looking at me.

"You can. I'd like...to hear you."

I wrap my arms around his torso and beam at him. "Because I'm your new boyfriend, I'll be happy to play for you. But I charge in kisses."

Logan chuckles, his breath dancing across my face. "Hey, I give those for free." We kiss, and those fireworks in my heart light up again.

After we pull apart, I sit down at the piano bench while he pulls up a rolling leather chair. "What do you wanna hear?"

"I don't know, something slow? A classic?" He shrugs and I realize the answer.

I start to play one of the earliest, most complex pieces I know. It's slow and delicate, but full of life towards the end, speeding up with complicated melodies. Before I can finish, I look over and see him hunched over, covering his mouth.

I stop playing. "What's wrong?"

"That's...that song..."

"I was playing 'Clair de Lune' by—"

"Debussy, I know, it's...it's beautiful. It's based on the poem by Verlaine, all about dance and love."

"Oh? You know it?"

"Yeah, my...my mom used to play the song all the time." A tear rolls down his face and I'm horrified to know I triggered him.

"Shit, I'm sorry." I get up, but he stops me by putting his hand on my knee.

"No, please, Wei." He looks up at me, his eyes both hurt and hopeful. "Please play it again."

I study his face carefully. I'm not certain, but I think he needs this. So, as he asked, we sit back down and I play it twice in a row, not stopping.

When I'm done, Logan is fast asleep in his armchair. I smile, knowing that I brought him peace. After a moment, he wakes up abruptly. "Shit, sorry, Wei."

"It's OK." I giggle. "I'll let you go to bed."

"Stay with me?"

"Are you sure you don't need your space?"

He stands up and confidently takes my hand and kisses it. "Not from you, no. Please, Wei, I want...to wake up with you."

Well how can I say no to that?

28: Logan

My eyes drift open in the morning, and I feel a warm body wrapped around me. I turn my head and see Wei is still asleep, breathing softly. He's wrapped me in his arms, and, even though he's half my bodyweight, I've never felt more safe. A big guy like me can probably defend himself in a fist fight, but that doesn't mean I can't get hurt. With Wei Wong in my life, the pain goes away.

He stirs and opens his eyes. "Morning," he yawns at me, stretching.

I smile. "Morning, baby." I grin and take his hand, lacing my fingers through his. "Did you sleep well?"

"Yeah." He chuckles. "Seeing you is a great way to wake up."

"Right back at ya. Did you...Was this a good first date?"

"It was a terrific first date." He bites his lip then looks down as if pondering. "I should get going soon, though."

"I understand." I nod, looking at the ceiling.

"But before I go..." I can hear the grin in his voice. "We can finish this date off...the best way I know how." Before I can ask, my hips thrust as he gently grabs my morning wood.

I shut my eyes, lick my lips, and moan. I reach over and grab his hardness well. I match him stroke for stroke, pulling back the sheet. Opening my eyes, I see him staring at me, hungry and desperate. His dick gets harder in my hand and his mouth is agape now.

"You're...so...sexy," he huffs. With my free hand, I reach over and tweak his nipple and it's game over for him. He shoots into my fist, moaning. Seeing him get off with me has me right on the edge. I lie back and enjoy his strokes. Right before I shoot, he leans over and catches my nipple with his mouth. It feels like every nerve in my body explodes as I come all over myself, shouting.

We spend the next few minutes lying there, catching our breaths. I'm relishing how perfect the morning and last night were, and how lucky I am to be here. I'm alive, in bed with a sexy man who makes me feel so good. I used to think all my best moments in life were behind me, but with Wei, life has meaning again.

After getting cleaned up, I drive Wei home since apparently he took a cab to my place so Pei could keep the car. "My sister's birthday is in a couple of weeks. I was thinking of taking you to dinner somewhere?"

"Sounds good." I park the car right in front of Wei's house.

"I still need to get her a gift," he mutters. "I want to get something novel, something not boring for once."

"A novelty gift, you say?" I scratch my chin. "I have an idea. When can you come shopping with me?"

Wei grins and shrugs. "Pei and I work a lot. Maybe next Friday?"

"Deal." I lean over and kiss him slowly, like I'm enjoying my favorite ice cream flavor. "God, I'll never get tired of kissing you."

"You sweet talk all the boys like this?" He kisses me again.

"Only one boy. My boyfriend. That sexy guy who works in the music department." We both chuckle in between kisses.

"Boyfriend. I like the sound of that." He gives my lips one last peck before he leaves my car. I don't drive away until I see he's gone inside.

♪

A few days later, as promised, I'm driving Wei to a nearby town.

"Where are you taking me?"

"Just trust me," I reply with a smirk. "My boyfriend is so impatient."

"Well, *my* boyfriend won't tell me where we're shopping." We both chuckle at this.

Five minutes and several turns later, we arrive at "Odd Shop by Otis" and I park right on the street. Wei looks perplexed as I lead him through the door. The store is packed to the walls with old furniture and other vintage items, big and small. From porcelain salt shakers to feather boas, if it's weird, you can find it here.

Otis walks up to us wearing his traditional plaid shirt. He's twenty-five years older than me, carries a larger, rounder frame, and has mostly gray hair with a matching thick mustache. "Logan Micucci," his voice booms. "Two visits in two months? To what do I owe this honor?"

Wei turns to me, and I beam at Otis. "The honor is all ours. Otis Pryor, meet Wei Wong. He's my um...boyfriend."

"Nice to meet you," Wei says, shaking Otis's hand.

"Likewise. It's nice to finally meet the person who's been taking up all of my Logan's time."

Wei turns to me. "Otis and my dad went way back," I tell him. Then I turn to Otis. "I never said I was dating someone."

"Ha! Please!" He chortles and walks behind the cash register. "It was written all over your face. The last time you came here you were so desperate for a lap harp. *'Oh Otis, I have to get one. It's sooo important.'*"

Wei turns to me, looking completely smug, and my cheeks burn. I look down and scratch my head. "I don't...That's not...I don't recall it like that."

"This old-timer knows a crush when he sees one. You forget, boy, I can read you like a book. Hell, I was there when you learned how to walk." Otis turns to Wei. "Something tells me you didn't only come here to embarrass Logan. What can I do ya for, Mr. Wong?"

Wei smiles at both of us. "My sister is turning thirty-two next week, and I was hoping for—"

"Creative gifts for the female members of your family, down that way." He points to a corridor and Wei nods and walks over. While he's there, I stay by the register and watch him peruse the shelves.

"I like him," Otis says in a lower tone.

"He's barely said two words to you."

"Doesn't matter. I call it like I see it, and I can tell he's a good man." I turn to Otis and see him studying Wei in the distance.

"What makes you say that?"

"I've never seen you as happy as the day I pulled that old harp out from storage for you." Otis turns and stares at me perceptively. "I can see how you feel about him. It's all over your face, whether you want to admit it or not."

"Admit what?"

"If someone can make you that happy, then they must be really special."

"It's...really new." I turn to see Wei looking at an old teapot. "But he is. Special to me."

"I'm just glad to see you getting out of the house."

"You don't care that I'm...dating a man? That I'm queer?" I never got to come out to my parents. I turn to see Otis staring down at his hands.

"When my wife died, I thought my life was over. I've seen that same look in your eyes for the past however-many years." My eyebrows furrow. I knew Otis's wife died, but he never talked about it. Truthfully, I never had any deep conversations with Otis, not even when my parents were alive.

"Your father is the one who told me that I needed to live again. He pulled me out of my slump like a best friend should. I want to do the same for you." He turns to me, and my eyes start to sting. "So take it from this old-timer: don't shy away from the world, Logan. If this Wong fellow makes you happy, then hold onto him. As the saying goes, '*love is love.*'"

I try to respond, but my throat is dry and I'm still fighting back the tears. There's so much I want to say. *Love? Really?*

"Your parents would be so proud of the man you've become." Before my heart can break, I spot Wei walking back to us, arms full of old knick-knacks. I turn my head to wipe away a stray tear while he lays it out on the cashier's desk.

"I couldn't decide!" Wei exclaims. "And I *had* to get something for my nephew."

"All good choices!" Otis chuckles while ringing him up. I make a mental note to visit this shop more often.

Love is love. Otis said he could see it on my face. I've never loved anyone I've dated before. Could it be I've fallen in love with Wei already?

29: Wei

Dating Logan and working at KU go together like fried eggs and rice. It turns out, when there's not a conflict of interest, it's very convenient having your boyfriend around. Felipe and I work closely with Professor Reyes, but since there are less students around in the summer, she gives us more room to be independent and grow as educators. I'm getting in plenty of practice on the harp, and the melodies and rhythms are becoming second nature to me.

I visit Logan in the Center constantly. The smiles on my face when I see him are only outmatched by his when he beams back at me. We're still trying to be discreet, but we sneak kisses in his office or when no one's around the fitness center. It's summer time, and most of the students are gone, so some days we have the whole building to ourselves.

Because it's summer, I pick up more shifts at my catering job. Logan and I haven't gotten to sleep together in a few weeks since my sister has been working, so I miss him. I knock on his office door to surprise him before lunch. "Hey!" I'm sure I have a dopey grin on my face; Logan has that effect on me. He smiles back at me as he swivels his chair.

"Hey you, what a sight for sore eyes."

"I figured I'd catch you for lunch?"

"Oof, I'm pretty swamped since a local summer camp is taking swimming lessons here later."

"Oh." My face falls in disappointment. He gets up and closes the door behind me and loudly locks it.

"But no one's around now," he growls, inches away from my face. My eyes widen, my cock takes interest, and my gaze flicks to his lips.

"Fuck, I'm so glad you have an office that's not in the Fine Arts building." Instantly, I assault his mouth with mine. He tastes so good, and when he kisses me back, my whole body ignites.

I swear, until the day I die, I will never get over kissing Logan Micucci.

While our lips battle for dominance, he guides my body to his desk. I hear the sounds of papers being pushed onto the floor. I pull back and look down, catching my breath. "Wow, are you sure you wanna mess up everything?"

"I've always wanted to do that." He grins and raises an eyebrow, and I just about melt. "Besides," he purrs. "This will make it easier for me to have my way with you." His hands travel up my knees to my inner groin and I get hard instantly.

"Right here?"

He kisses my neck, and my eyes shut. "Right now."

Ah, fuck it. "OK," I reply, my voice a breathy whisper.

He strokes my erection through my jeans, then

unbuttons me. After unzipping me, I lift up so he can yank my pants down. The desk is cold on my ass, but how can I care when this perfect man is kneeling in front of me?

"Can I take care of you, Wei?"

"Only if you take your shirt off." Ever the obedient soldier, he smiles then shucks it off. "Oh fuck, you're beautiful babe." Chiseled, shirtless Logan is best Logan—my head can't properly grammar right now.

He leans in and licks one long stripe up my throbbing cock. I hiss in pleasure and put my hands on his shoulders. When he moves further and takes me in, I fall backward, hands on the desk.

I'm lost in a galaxy of euphoria as he sucks me off. My hand is aching since it's digging into his keyboard, but I don't fucking care. Every time I open my eyes, I see Logan's chiseled frame bobbing up and down. He's pleasing me; he's worshipping my cock, all for my satisfaction. The thought of it sends me so close to the edge.

"Logan…I…" I thread my hands in his hair, and he hums, knowing what's to come—me, I'm what's to come.

I grunt and shoot into him, and he swallows all of me, every last drop. Once I'm breathing normally again, I open my eyes and look down. Logan is staring at me, jerking off while on his knees.

"Do you want me to service you, babe?" I ask.

In lieu of a response, or as a response, he rolls his eyes back and grunts. He shoots onto the floor, and I can't believe this stud had an orgasm just looking at me. *What is my life now?*

Once we've recovered, Logan cleans up the mess on the floor with his undershirt and some spare wipes he had lying around.

"Thanks for that," he murmurs into my lips as he holds my head and kisses me.

"I should be thanking you."

"Nah, it was all my pleasure. But I gotta get back to work here." He winks and turns me around. Then after I unlock the door, he gives me a firm pat on the ass and I yelp.

We're both giggling by the time I walk out the door. I almost bump into Aggie, clad in her signature pink sweatband on her head.

"Oh, Wei, what brings you here?"

"I um…" I turn to see Logan leaning against his doorframe.

"He was…asking me for…exercise techniques."

"That's right!" I nod three times for good measure. "Um, exercise techniques."

Aggie stares at both of us, an eyebrow raised. "Uh-huh. Well, I'm going to *actually* exercise, unlike you two." I turn to leave when I hear her say, "Also, your fly's open, Wei."

I hear Logan chuckle as I zip up and wipe the sweat from my brow. Before I leave, I overhear Aggie say "Stargazing worked like a charm, I see."

30: Logan

I ring the doorbell and, after a moment, it opens. "Hey, Penny. Or should I call you Pei?"

"It's whatever you prefer." She lets me in and puts on her coat. "Look, I'm in a rush, but Wei will be out soon. I'm sorry this is so last minute." I walk into the entrance hallway, but before I can ask her what she's talking about, the door closes and she's gone.

I hear the sound of steps in another room, so I decide to wait. Looking around, I see some letters on the side table. Some of them are addressed to a "Ms. Lynette Fa Guo." This must be the aunt who abandoned Wei and Pei. Just the thought of a parental figure leaving on purpose upsets me. The fact that Wei, the most incredible, talented, and generous person I've ever met, had to be without a parent all this time...makes my blood boil. I make a mental note that I need to fix this.

Before I can continue that train of thought, Wei walks in. He's wearing a light-blue button-down and a black hoodie; no matter what outfit he wears, he takes my breath away.

"Hey, babe." I hope he doesn't mind me saying that.

"I'm so *so* sorry Logan."

"What's wrong?"

"I know we were supposed to have a date at a restaurant tonight, but—"

"I'm not hungry, Uncle Wei!" Galen's little feet pitter-patter into view. "Logan! You're here!"

"Hey, little man!"

"Pei had to work another night shift. I should have called but I've been so busy." He frowns and turns to his nephew. "You need to eat something for dinner. You barely touched lunch."

"But Uncle Wei!" he whines.

"It's no problem!" I blurt, trying to head off a family argument. They both turn to me. "Why don't we three go out to dinner?"

"Yay!" Galen cheers.

"I couldn't accept that."

"Hey, you promised me dinner and a movie. Why can't the three of us go?" I ask.

"A movie?" Galen's eyes light up.

Wei looks down, biting his lip. "It *is* early…"

"I love movies!" Galen chimes in.

"Are you sure it's OK? We were supposed to have our…" Wei's voice trails off. He's trying to apologize for screwing up our date night, but I don't mind in the slightest.

"Your what?" Galen asks.

"It's not a problem. You, me, and the little man here can go to dinner and a movie. I think there's a new kid's show playing. That'd be fun!"

"Can we, Uncle Wei?"

"Please," I suggest to Galen.

"Please?" Galen echoes.

Wei looks at both of us. "I haven't been to the movies in forever." He shrugs, then looks down. "Go to the bathroom first then get your coat."

"Yay!" Galen cheers as he runs off. As soon as he's gone, Wei walks up to me.

"I owe you big time."

"Nonsense. What was that currency? Getting paid in kisses?" I grin, and he leans up to kiss me, softly.

"You get those for free." Wei smiles at me and I feel my heart getting dangerously close to the "L-word" that Otis mentioned.

After I load up the spare child seat for Galen, we hit the road to the multiplex. "So, I've been meaning to ask you." Wei turns to me. "What's your sister's actual name? Is it Penny?"

"It's Pei. But she adjusted it to make an 'American English' nickname." He uses air-quotes then continues. "Kids were annoying her at school, and my aunt didn't help when she came home all sad. She wasn't one to console us."

I grimace and grip the steering wheel harder. Kids made fun of them and their aunt, their only family, didn't support them? That thought fills me with fury. I want to tell Wei's aunt to fuck off on his behalf. If my parents were alive and they'd left me, I'd find them to give them a piece of my mind.

Maybe I can help Wei find his family. If he's willing, perhaps it's not too late for him to repair his relationship with his aunt. There might be more to his family situation than he realizes, but he won't know unless he reaches out. He has an opportunity that I don't, and I don't want Wei to squander it.

After a minute, I finally reply "School kids can be cruel. What about you? You've always been 'Wei'?"

"Yup. I didn't bother changing it." He shrugs. "My sister supported me, but I didn't want to sacrifice my name for the sake of others. I had so little growing up. My name was the only thing I had."

"So true."

"Kids were going to make fun of me for being Chinese in upstate New York no matter what. My sister taught me that." He shrugs again, and my heart breaks even further.

"That's...awful. You shouldn't have had to go through any of that."

"Yeah, well... it wasn't just the kids." I look over and see him gazing out the window. "Dating is never easy. When you're Asian, so many people in this country disqualify you from the dating pool, like you don't count."

"That's not true," I reply in a reflex. But no, I can't dismiss his experiences. "Well, I never thought of that."

"Being a person of color is something I have to be acutely aware of at all times." He turns to me and glances back at Galen. "Especially when dating in *our* community."

I knew bullshit like that existed in the LGBTQ

realm, but I'd never had to deal with it. He looks at me expectantly, so I try to pick my next words carefully. "Well… I like you. Not because of your race, not despite your race, but because of everything you are."

Wei smiles at me and puts his hand on my knee. If the kid wasn't here, I'm sure he would have leaned in and kissed me.

"I like you both!" Galen chirps. "And my gym teacher, he lets me play soccer. And I like the other kids in my class who are good at soccer!" Wei and I chuckle as I continue my drive to the theater.

Once we arrive, we decide to eat at the multiplex food court. We share chicken tenders, hot dogs, and fries while we attempt to convince Galen to eat. After dinner, we go to watch a big-screen animated movie, some film about two fish-monster boys who go on a kid-friendly adventure. Little man wants to sit between us, and I assure Wei I don't mind.

The entire time, my left hand lies on top of Galen's chair and Wei's right hand reaches mine. We keep our hands intertwined, and we play with each other's fingers during the movie. No one's behind us and Galen doesn't seem to notice, so we're in our own little world. I can't say what happened in the film; I was too busy glancing at Wei and sharing secret smiles. Just like when we hang out, the two of us, or when we sleep together, a voice inside my head tells me how perfect it all feels.

Being with his family feels right, like all the pieces I've been missing for six years are falling into place, and I could really *really* get used to this.

{

Two days later, I walk through the KU library doors and spot a student worker at a desk. As I cross the large entranceway to her, I try to suppress any nagging feelings of guilt. I didn't tell Wei of my plan, but I'm sure he'll thank me. Eventually. He has to be grateful, right?

"Hi, how can I be of assistance?"

"Hi, um, I was wondering if you could help me do a wider search on one of the PC's? I tried at home, but to no avail."

"Certainly!" She pushes up her red-framed glasses, then gets up. "What book are you looking for?"

"Not a book...I'm...doing research." My throat goes dry around the lie I'm telling. "I want to, um, interview someone. I'm looking for one person in particular."

31: Wei

Dating Logan this summer has been heavenly. He's amazing, and being around him makes me feel all warm and light, like the sun is always shining on me just the right amount. He fits in with my family, who are the most important part of my life. He loves listening to me talk about music, and I've never felt beautiful before I met him. The sex is awesome, and I've been able to sleep over a couple of times. When Galen asks where I'm going I simply tell him I have nighttime work and my sister makes sure he doesn't ask any more pressing questions.

Waking up with Logan in my arms feels like perfection. I've slept over at a guy's place maybe twice in the past seven years; hook-ups don't usually want me to stick around, and the feeling has been mutual. With Logan, I can see myself waking up in his arms for a long time.

It's frightening, but with every kiss, every cute text, and every genuine smile, I know for sure I'm falling for him. I've never loved anyone like this before, so I'm scared beyond measure.

I'm not going to let my fears sabotage my

burgeoning relationship, so I'll take it day-by-day. A fantastic summer with a hot guy in my arms? I think I finally deserve this.

As the season winds down, so does my semester of study at KU. I'm performing today with the other music department grad students as the culmination of a summer's worth of study. I'm surprised by the turnout; I presume they're mostly family members, but it's still a decent number. Professor Reyes has arranged for lots of refreshments out in the hallway for when we're done.

Peeking out from behind the curtain, I spot Logan chatting with Galen and Pei in the second row. Seeing him act like a surrogate fun uncle for Galen makes me fall for him even harder, and my face feels warm as I walk back behind the curtain.

The show is going well so far, with Felipe and three other grad students playing their respective instruments during their sets. Once I get on stage, I try to breathe slowly to calm myself. All of my music teachers have said I carry poise and confidence, but like a lot of performers, I'm faking it 'til I can make it.

It's so quiet I swear I can hear my heartbeat as I walk across the stage. I get up to the harp, take a seat, pull it down to my shoulder, and put my fingers where I know I'm going to be starting. I'm almost ready to play when I spot someone I recognize in the audience way in the back row.

No.

Is that my aunt?

It can't be. No.

I must be seeing things. My pulse starts racing. What is Aunt Lynette doing here? No, it has to be an illusion. But what if it *is* her? No, she would never. She never came to my recitals as a teen. She left us. She never wanted to be our parent. Why would she care enough to watch me play?

Before I can start panicking, I see Professor Reyes in the backstage area. She's looking at me, eyebrows raised, almost as if to say, *"What are you waiting for, Wei?"*

That's right; I'm here in the Korham U Fine Arts building. There are thirty-plus people in the audience ready to watch me play. I shake my head a little and breathe in. No one else is here; it's just me and the harp. As I exhale, my mind visualizes the air leaving my lungs, and I calm down a bit. I feel the strings on the tips of my fingers. The wires are taut with tension, and with each pluck, a note will reverberate, giving birth to music. I know what string to play first, then second, then where my hands need to go next.

I see the entire song in my head; just like the piano pieces I've mastered, it's simply notes in a certain sequence. It's chords, arpeggios, simple melodies, complex rhythms, and the occasional glissando. It's music, the one thing I've always excelled at. I've got this.

And so I play.

My song goes well and everyone applauds. After the other grad students and I do a group bow, Reyes comes out and shares some final words about how proud she is of the music department. She directs the audience to the massive refreshments table outside, but I'm not listening. I gaze intently at that face in the back.

It's definitely my Aunt Lynette; she has shorter hair and glasses, but it's her. What she's doing here, I don't know, but I'll be damned if I let her walk into our life again so easily. When most of the audience leaves for the snack table, I see her walk out the opposite door. Perfect, I don't want her meeting Galen or Logan, and I need to confront her on my own.

I move quickly once I walk out of the theater. "*Ye Yi!*" I call my aunt by one of the few Chinese words we picked up over the years. She stops, then turns around; in this hallway, it's just me, her, and light streaming through the massive, walled windows. I stop a couple of meters in front of her, afraid if I get too close an old wound will pop open. I don't say anything. I look her in the eye, my fists clenched in anger, waiting for her to explain herself.

"Wei. You've...grown." She sounds as cold as ever.

"Why are you *here*?" I ask, my jaw clenched. It's been almost eight years. I think of the days I worked double-shifts, the nights staying up with baby Galen, the long bus rides between jobs, the arduous journey of teaching myself how to do taxes, and my pulse rises. She should have been here for the past eight years. The question I should have asked is *"Where have you been?"*

"I...wanted to see your performance." She's studying me, like I'm an animal who might pounce. "You did...quite well."

"I don't *need* your approval!" I bark, unable to control my own voice. She flinches and I close my eyes. *One breath in, and one breath out.* "How did you even find out about this?" My fists continue to clench, but my voice is calm again.

"Your friend said I needed to see you," she replies, visibly confused.

What?

What is she talking about? What friend? "He said you were ready to hear me out and make amends."

"I don't know if you hit your head, but I never said any of that. You've lost it, *Ye Yi.*"

I turn around to leave, this time never to see her again, but she speaks up. "I don't know why you're mad. Logan emailed me saying you wanted me to come."

I flinch and turn back around. "OK, now I *know* you're definitely lying." I point at her, fury in my voice. "Logan would never do that. So you can—"

"She's not." I whip my head around and see Logan standing there. He looks hurt, and his eyes are wet. "She's not lying. I emailed her."

What?

All the blood drains from my face. "I emailed her about your performance," he says. I search his face and I try to make it all make sense. My boyfriend...the man I've been falling for...did this to me?

I turn back to my aunt who looks more confused than either of us. "Could you give us a minute?" I manage to ask while my blood boils.

She shakes her head. "You two need to talk this over. I get it. Goodbye, Wei." She leaves through the one exit, and I turn back around to Logan, my jaw clenched.

"What. Did you. *Do?*"

He looks worried, like he might break apart, but I don't even care. "I found your aunt online, and I um...I thought..."

"You thought what?"

"That you needed to talk to her/"

"Who said I needed that?" I shout at him, unable to contain my rage. I point at him, still a yard away. "Why. Why. *Why* would you think that?"

"Because I see it every time you talk about her!" He sounds desperate.

I run my hands through my hair and look around in frustration. "Logan, I've told you a hundred times, I don't want to talk about the *one* person in my life who left us when we needed her! Why would you think I'd want to see her in person? Do you have *any* idea how it feels to be...to be blindsided like this? I've finally made a name for myself. I don't need her!"

"I know you think you're OK, but if you could just patch up your issues—" He steps forward, but I step back.

"Oh my God! Logan! I *don't* want to see her! She never even wanted to be our parent. Don't you understand that we're *fine* without her?" My voice is starting to crack and my eyes are tearing up. I've never felt this betrayed in my life.

"Yes, but Wei, if you talk to her, then maybe you can be a family again."

"And *you* get to make that decision? What the hell, Logan? You are *NOT* part of this *FAMILY!*" I shout.

He flinches and stares at me open-mouthed. My words hang heavy in the air. Neither of us makes a sound. Logan stares at me, moisture beginning to form in his eyes.

Maybe I crossed a line, maybe he did, too, but our silence has made it clear this conversation is over. His face is filled with so much hurt that I need to look down as I stride past him down the hallway and turn the corner.

Finally, I reach the large crowd where everyone is still congregating and having snacks. I see happy families congratulating their sons and daughters. *Gee, I wonder what that's like? Aunt Lynette never did that for me.*

After way too long, I walk up to Pei and Galen, who are chatting with Felipe while they eat cookies. "Hey, we need to go."

"Uh, OK." Pei seems to sense my urgency. "It was nice meeting you."

"Same to you," Felipe replies. He pushes his glasses up and looks at me. "Congrats, man, you did great."

"Yeah, you too," I mutter, still not strong enough to look up.

I lead Pei and Galen out as quickly as I can and turn off my phone. Once we get settled in the car, Pei starts driving, and I look out the window; no signs of Aunt Lynette or Logan, so that's good.

"Are you alright, Brother?"

"I'm fine."

I can sense she doesn't believe me, but I can't talk about it —not yet.

"I got two chocolate chip cookies, Uncle Wei. You want one?" Galen asks with his little voice.

Gazing out the window at the trees as we pass by, I simply reply, "No, kiddo, they're all yours."

32: Logan

"Sorry, I'm unable to answer the phone. Please leave your name, number, and the reason why you're calling, and I'll get back to you as soon as I can." The phone leaves a loud beeping noise, and I take a deep breath.

"Hey Wei, it's me...Logan." I close my eyes and put my hand on my forehead. "Listen, I don't know if you got my other messages...or if you really have blocked me or...if your phone isn't working or something but...in case you didn't, I just want to say..."

I look up at the ceiling and take another breath. "I'm sorry." I turn off my phone and place it on my desk. I walk out of my office, my footsteps echoing through the empty building.

I make my way to the closed coffee kiosk where I saw him in January. I peer at the front door where mistletoe dangled on that fateful December night. I gaze past the window toward the Fine Arts building, several yards away up a hill. I could go there looking for him, but I don't think classes are in session for the next two weeks.

Besides, even if he is there, he's made it abundantly clear

he doesn't want to see me. It's been five days and countless texts and voicemails; if he wanted to talk to me, he would have.

Frankly, if I were in his shoes, I wouldn't want to talk to me either.

I sigh and go back to my desk and spin in my chair, looking up. When my parents died, I asked the universe why it hated me, why it would do this to me because I didn't deserve it.

But this? I deserve this.

Later that day, I walk through the front door of "Odd Shop by Otis".

"Logan! Back already?" Otis asks, sauntering to the front area from the back room.

"Uh...yeah..." My voice is breaking, trying to hold back my emotions.

Otis eyes me warily. "Did you...need to buy something?"

"Um..." I look around and grab the nearest knick-knack. "Yes. I came here for...this."

"Why do you need a silver lipstick and powder holder?" I open up the trinket and find it is, indeed, a fancy container for make-up.

"Um...I don't know." I put it down and take a deep breath.

"Uh-huh." I see him studying me, so I look around, not wanting to meet his gaze. "How did the gifts work out for

Wei and his family?"

"Great."

"How's he doing?"

"He's great, too." I stare out the window, unable to lie any longer. "Actually I don't know why I said that. He's...really mad at me." I fight back tears as I stare out at the street. "Otis, I fucked up."

"Aw, Logan." Otis pushes a gilded tissue box holder to me. "Come on. Tell me what's really on your mind."

I take a tissue and dab my eyes. "Sorry to dump all my drama on you, I just...I don't have too many friends that don't work at KU so..."

"Never apologize for opening up to me," he says in his booming voice. "You tell me all your shit because your father and I did the same thing, God rest his soul. I swore I would be there for you, and now that you're ready, you can tell me anything."

I smile through my tears. My heart feels warmer knowing Otis is willing to support me the way he used to be there for my dad. "I...went behind Wei's back. I contacted his estranged family member, even though he told me not to, hoping he would want to see them again. But he didn't, and it hurt him. *I* hurt him." I look at the ground. "I shouldn't have done that, and now he won't talk to me."

"Oh kid...I'm sorry you're hurting right now."

"I...don't know what to do."

"When my late wife used to get mad at me, I had the privilege of living with her, knowing she'd come home eventually."

I look up at him. "But I don't—"

"Is this Wei fellow a good guy?"

"Yeah?" I'm not sure what he's getting at. "He's the best

person I know."

"Then he'll find you when he's ready."

"Then what do I—"

"Be ready with all of the apologies and explanations you can muster. That's what my wife and I did, and we loved each other until the day she died."

I nod, ruminating on his words.

"OK." I sniff. "Thanks, Otis." I turn to leave but his voice stops me.

"Oh and, Logan, don't forget step one."

"What's that?"

"Hurting someone you love is like hurting yourself. So, step one: Forgive yourself." He smiles and nods sagely at me and I feel better already.

33: Wei

My sister puts down two cups of coffee while I sit at our kitchen table. I'm fiddling on my phone and I don't even bother to look at her. At last, she breaks the silence. "Are you finally ready to talk to me?"

"Are you going to let it go if I say no?" I rub my temple and breathe in the smell of sweet caffeine. It's 5:50 in the morning, and Pei is getting ready for work. I haven't been sleeping well, and the bags under my eyes give it away.

"Well, you can talk to me, or you can call him. Those are your choices."

I groan and take the cup. I have a sip, and it's still hot, so I smack my lips. It's dark, bitter, and hurts my mouth, so it's perfect. "Not sure what you're getting at."

She rolls her eyes. "OK, I guess I'm going to have to grill you. What happened at the recital? Since you haven't gone out and I haven't seen Logan, I can guess it has something to do with him."

I shrug, knowing if I start talking my emotions will make me crazy. I'm hurt and betrayed, but I'm not sure who to be mad at more, Logan or myself. My sister continues, "You also look like your heart's been stomped on." My eyes dart up to see her staring intently at her cup. "I know what that feels like. It's been some time for me, and I've never seen it on you, which means you must really be in love with him."

I scoff, looking back down. "Maybe I was."

"Feelings like that don't just disappear in a week. He was so, *so* proud of you during your recital."

My eyes dart up. "He was?" I ask quickly.

"Oh my God, Brother," she scoffs. "I looked over at him while you were playing, and I swear he was two seconds away from jumping on stage and groping you." I can't help the smile on my lips. "A guy like that doesn't come into your life often. Now please, before Galen gets up, tell me what happened."

I take a deep breath and look back down at the table. My finger plays with a spilled droplet of coffee. "He called Aunt Lynette. Well, he emailed her. She was at the showcase."

"What?"

"Apparently, Logan felt I needed to patch things up with her *so badly* that he went ahead and tracked her down. I confronted her after the concert and she told me Logan emailed her behind my back. God, I *told* Logan not to contact her *so* many times, but he did it anyway. He claimed it was so we could be a family again." I close my eyes and take another burning sip. I let the aroma of coffee and the void of silence fill the kitchen for a few seconds while my sister processes it all.

"That's...wow."

"I know," I reply. "I've never felt that hurt before."

"What'd you say to *Ye Yi*?"

"Almost nothing. She left, of course, but I was so, *so* mad at

Logan."

"Jeez…" We both sip coffee while she takes it all in. "She actually came to one of your concerts, huh? That's a first."

My eyebrows scrunch up. "Can we please focus on the real problem here?"

"Which is…?"

I look at her incredulously and wave my hand around. "Logan. Betraying me."

"I take it you haven't talked to him since?"

"What part of 'betrayal' don't you understand?"

"The part where he's in love with you." My heart skips a beat. Could that be true? No one's ever told me they loved me that way.

"Look," my sister continues. "What Logan did was… wrong. Probably. He shouldn't have gone behind your back."

"What do you mean 'probably'?"

She ignores me and continues. "But you should give him a chance to explain himself or apologize. Look at it from his perspective for like, thirty seconds please? Is there any reason why he'd want so badly for you, the guy he's known for *less than a year*, to be reunited with his long-lost aunt?"

I stare at my lap, guilt washing over me. "His…parents died a few years ago and he has no one to call his family."

"Ah…now it all makes sense." She gets up to put away her mug.

"But that doesn't excuse what he did."

"Maybe not," she replies, washing the cup. "Doesn't mean it didn't come from a loving place. And it doesn't mean he doesn't care about you deeply. I'd do anything to have a guy like that in my life."

I frown. I keep forgetting my sister has probably been as celibate and lonely as I have. She walks over to me and gives me a pat on the shoulder. "Logan might not have a family, but we do. He found our aunt. Maybe there's something there, and we actually can be a family again. Either way, you should go talk to Logan. He's someone who's become important to Galen's life, and yours."

"I...don't know if I'm ready yet, or if he'll even still want to be with me. I told him he wasn't part of our family. I could tell it hurt him."

"Ah, but you want him to be?"

I shrug. "I don't know yet. It's all so soon. I can't even patch things up with *Ye Yi*. How can I let someone else into our family?"

"Only you can answer that question. But talking to Logan is a good way to start."

"I'll think about it." I nod and she walks away. "And thanks Sister. Love you lots."

"Love you too, Brother."

Yawning, I walk into the living room and sit down on our small couch, too tired to make it downstairs. I think about building a better future for Galen and how much he loves Logan as a surrogate uncle. Maybe it's the tiredness talking, but I know I love him, too. Before I can text him, sleep overtakes me.

I wake up to the sunlight on my face and immediately check my phone; apparently I dozed off for about an hour. I walk to Galen's room and notice the blanket is undone, so he must be out of bed.

I go to the bathroom, but he's not there. The house is unusually quiet. "Galen?" I holler.

He's not in his room, my sister's room, or the bathroom. It's a Saturday morning; he should be sitting at the kitchen table eating cereal, but instead, I spy a large piece of paper on our table.

My pulse starts to race. In Galen's hand-writing in crayon, it reads, *"Going to find family. Be back later. Galen."*

All the blood leaves my face and I run to the front door. It's unlocked, meaning someone walked out after my sister left. *Shit.*

I open the door and look left and right. The sun is shining, but no one is around. *"Galen!"* I shout to the world, but there's no response.

My nephew, my whole world, has run away.

34: Logan

I haven't been sleeping much since Wei ghosted me—for good reason, I understand it, but still. We had a good thing going, and I blew it. The crazy thing is, I was falling in love with him. I could see a future for us: him playing the piano and me sitting next to him, perpetually smiling. He could move in, I'd use my inheritance to buy him a real harp, he'd eventually become the head of the music department at KU, and we'd drive Galen off to college—the whole works. But that's a big future to hope for with someone I hurt so badly.

I walk over to my music room and put my hand on the piano my mom used to play. I open it up and trace a few keys with my finger. Just because Wei is probably breaking up with me doesn't mean I can't learn music, right? I play one key, then another, then a third. They make a chord, and it's in harmony, like I learned. I sigh and try to ignore the ache in my heart.

Suddenly, my phone vibrates in my pocket. Who's calling me so early in the morning?

Wei?

"Hello, Wei?"

"Logan…it's Galen…and I need…*Shit*…I need help! I can't find…I have no one else I can call! My sister is at work and… *shit*…" It's him, alright, but there's a panic in his voice I've never heard before.

"Wei? Wei, just breathe. I'm here…tell me what's wrong."

I hear a deep breath on the line. "Galen's run away from home. My sister went to work early, taking the car. I took a nap for like an hour…When I woke up, the front door was unlocked. *Shit*, it was just an hour, and now he's nowhere in the house. I looked everywhere. I don't have a car. He could get hurt. Someone could kidnap him. Who knows what could happen!" I can tell he's crying.

Fuck, Galen ran away? If anything were to happen to the boy…

"I'm on my way. Stay put."

"OK…" He doesn't sound convinced and he sounds like he's still sobbing.

"Breathe for me, Wei. I'll be there in five minutes and I promise we'll find him."

"Alright…Thank you." He sniffs and hangs up. I get dressed faster than I thought humanly possible.

When I imagined Wei calling me back, never in a thousand years did I think it would happen like this. I have so many things I need to tell him.

But first, we need to find Galen.

* * *

As I drive to Wei's house, I keep an eye out on the side of the road. It's a good thing too, because otherwise I would have missed the small person in a familiar little beanie hat. After I cross the bridge over Dugan's Brook, I spot Galen sitting on a tree stump, hunched over and looking defeated. I park on the side of the road, and once I realize he's just sitting there, I call Wei.

"Hello, Logan. Are you still coming?"

"Hey, yes, I was on my way and I found him. He seems fine, just sitting here."

"You found Galen? Where is he?"

"Near the bridge over Dugan's Brook on the way to your house. Do you want me to—"

"Stay with him. I'm coming." Before I can argue—it's like a fifteen minute walk from his place—the line goes dead.

I walk up to Galen, and he looks up in panic at my approach. I think it's a "*stranger danger*" thing, so, it's good he has some self-preservation reflex.

I wave a hand sheepishly, so as not to spook him. "Hey little man."

"Logan!" He sounds so happy, and I'm overjoyed to confirm that, yes, Galen is all in one piece. "You found me!"

"Yes I did. Are you alright?"

"I'm fine."

"OK. Wanna tell me what you're doing out here all alone?"

He looks down, guilt written all over his face. "I was looking for you."

"For me?"

"I heard you lived across the brook. But then I got scared of crossing the bridge. And then I forgot how to get home. So I sat here on this stump." He hops back up on the stump and looks down, defeated again.

"Why were you looking for me?" I sit down next to him.

"Because I heard Uncle Wei talking to Mommy this morning. He said you weren't part of our family." Galen's voice starts to quiver, but I hold my breath. *How do I take care of a crying child?* "But I want you to be part of our family." He looks up at me, eyes wet.

"Oh, little man." I look out at the road, uncomfortable with this small human crying next to me. "It's complicated. Grown-up life and families are not simple." I'm distressed knowing Wei told his sister about how I royally messed up, but I need to be strong for Galen. "You ran away to convince me to join your family?" I ask him gently.

"No. I know you wanna be in our family." He glances up at me, a hopeful look on his cute little face. "I can tell because you're always so smiley when you look at Uncle Wei and he's not looking at you." I try to fight the grin of embarrassment. Even a seven-year-old can tell how bad I have it for Wei. "But Uncle Wei said he's not sure if you wanna talk to him again."

"What?"

"He said he doesn't know if you would talk to him again or how to let people into our family. But he's been so sad ever since you stopped talking to him for *five whole days*." He takes out his fingers to count. "No, *six* whole days. So if I found you, I thought I could ask you to talk to him."

My heart wants to burst; if a fraction of what this kid is saying is true, then Wei misses me too.

"But I got lost and scared. And now Uncle Wei is gonna hate me for running away." He's on the verge of tears again, so I put my hand on his shoulder.

"Oh Galen, that's really sweet of you. But like I said, grown-up talk is complicated. You shouldn't have run away. But I know, beyond a shadow of a doubt, your Uncle Wei will be happy to see you. He'll hug you so hard your hat will fall off."

That earns me a smile. "What's 'beyond a shadow of a doubt'?"

Oh God, I have to teach a little kid English terms? "It means...when you're sure of something."

"OK." That seems to suffice and we sit there quietly for a bit, his little legs swinging.

"Uncle Logan?"

"Yes," I reply before realizing what he said. *Holy shit, I'm Uncle Logan?*

"Will you play football and soccer with me, even if Uncle Wei doesn't marry you?"

"What...even if...what?"

"I know he wants to marry you, because he looks at you the way they do in cartoons when they fall in 'love.' But if he doesn't, will you still play sports with me?"

There's so much to process in that sentence I don't know where to begin. So instead, I smile and pat him on the shoulder again. "If your mom and uncle are fine with it, I'll teach you all about whatever sports you want, kiddo."

35: Wei

The relief I feel seeing Galen in one piece is immeasurable. I run up to him and throw my arms around his little body, nearly sobbing in relief.

"Uncle Wei, you're squishing me." I let out a laugh-and-sob combination, then let him go. I hold his head in my hands and look him over.

"Are you OK? How long were you gone? Are you cold? Or hot? Are you hurt?"

"I'm fine, Uncle Wei," he mutters. "But you're squishing me still."

I smile and hug him one more time, then let go. Since I basically sprinted over here after Logan called me, I take a moment to catch my breath. I turn to Logan, and an odd mixture of emotions pools into my chest. I feel apologetic, still resentful, horny—because *damn, he looks good*—but most of all, grateful he found Galen before some stranger could get him.

Then, my concern rises up again, and I turn back to my nephew. "How could you leave? Do you have any idea how scared I was? You could have gotten hurt!"

"I'm sorry." He looks up at me with his adorable eyes and a pout that seems so genuine. His seven-year-old cuteness disarms me, making it impossible for me to stay mad at him.

"It's alright." I turn back to Logan and my mouth is suddenly dry.

He nods, seeming to understand. "I can give you two a ride home. If you'd like. Or I can leave, whichever you prefer." He lifts his hands up and takes a step back.

"A ride home...would be nice." I gaze into his beautiful eyes. Fuck, there's so much we need to talk about. "Thank you. So much."

"It was nothing. If the roles were reversed, I'd like to think you'd help me." I smile and take Galen by the hand to Logan's car.

"Can I share my dinosaur nuggets with Uncle Logan when we get home?" Galen asks.

I don't miss the blush on Logan's face at hearing this. I smile at my nephew. "Only if he wants some."

He's Uncle Logan now? Something about that makes my insides feel fuzzy.

When we get home, I invite Logan to stay for lunch, and he accepts. There's a tension between us because of all the issues we need to resolve, but today, I'm just happy Galen's OK. I prepare lunch while Logan entertains Galen by watching cartoons with him. It means a lot that, despite what transpired, he's still here supporting me. Seeing him be so caring with my nephew, I know my feelings for him haven't disappeared, they've only grown. I can only hope we can work through whatever issues we have going on.

After lunch, I help Galen take a bath, then take a nap. I watch him in the doorway for a bit longer before returning to the kitchen. To my pleasant surprise, Logan did the dishes. Little gestures like this make me envision a domestic future with him, but we need to get through the now first.

"Thanks for cleaning up." He looks up and grins at me, and the butterflies swirl around my stomach. "And... for saving my nephew."

"I didn't save him." He wipes his hands on a towel. "I simply happened to find him. But like I said, it's not a problem. Anything for the little man."

I pull out chairs for both of us, and we sit down. "It's just...I'll be forever grateful. He's my whole world. My family is...everything to me." He looks at me with concern in his eyes. *Here goes nothing.*

Logan opens his mouth to talk, but I interrupt him. "I'm sorry about last week."

"Why are *you* sorry?" he asks, clearly puzzled. "I'm the one who ruined everything we had."

"Had?"

"I...assume this is a breakup conversation?" His eyes hold a mixture of fear and hope.

"What? No." I shake my head. "But...if you can't forgive me for the way I...blew up, I can understand."

"Uh, I'll forgive you if you can forgive *me*!" he says, grinning.

"Really?" My mouth starts to twitch upward, and his eyes brighten.

"Yeah!" Logan laughs. "Will you forgive me? I was such an *ass*, and it was wrong of me to go behind your back and call your aunt. I'm *so* sorry, and I swear, I'll never do anything like that again."

"How can I *not* forgive you, even if you hadn't found Galen?" I chuckle. "Logan, I still care about you. This past week of not talking to you I've barely slept, but I needed time to process what happened. That's why I didn't call you back. I was going to today, I swear. I don't want this stupid fight to get between us." My heart is beating out of my chest as I reach for his hand across the table. "So what do you say? No more secrets?"

"None, I promise."

"OK. So, are we back on?"

His smile is dazzling as he puts his hand in mine. "If I kissed you right now, would that answer your question?"

I smile and lean in slowly, and his lips meet me halfway. Logan feels like the part of me I never knew I was missing. I feel like I'm whole now. I moan as a symphony of emotions rings through my heart, and I swear I'll never push this man away again.

185

* * *

"Are you sure you want to do this?" Logan asks. I'm at his house today. I filled Pei in on the drama from yesterday, the highs and the lows, and she insisted I have lunch with my boyfriend. "I know you were really upset when I contacted her."

I smile and pull him in for a tender kiss, just because I can. When I pull back, his eyes flutter in a daze and he smiles back. "I'm sure, babe," I reply, and his face gets redder. I turn to his laptop, which is in front of me on his kitchen table. "I was blindsided that day, but I've had a lot of time to think it over. Pei made me realize your actions came from a loving place."

Shit, did I say love? Logan doesn't seem to react, so I continue. "And now, I think I'm ready. To webcam chat with her." I look over at him, and he nods solemnly. "Here goes." I press the button dramatically.

Aunt Lynette and I emailed and agreed on a time to chat, so I know she'll pick up. I'm holding my breath during those three rings on the PC, but eventually her face pops up.

"Hello?" she says.

"Hello, *Ye Yi*, can you hear me?" I wave, and Logan cranes his head into the camera.

"Hi, yes." She adjusts her camera. She appears to be in a plain living room. "Hi there, Wei. Hi, um, are you Logan?"

"Hi." He chuckles awkwardly and waves.

"Um, so..." she says. "You probably have a lot you want to say."

I've imagined this moment for years, but I never thought it would actually happen. Now that it's here, I'm frozen. I glance at Logan, and he puts his hand on my knee. He's here for me, ready to support me in any way.

"Well, actually..." I shrug. "I just wanted to ask how you are. How's...life?"

Logan and Aunt Lynette both look at me in surprise. "I'm well. Busy working, always."

"Of course. Same here."

"How's your sister?"

"She and Galen are doing well."

"Galen is...her son?"

"Yup." We both smile and nod, unsure of where to go next with this conversation.

"You did very well at the concert."

"Thanks. I'm a music professor at KU now."

"Wow, that is quite impressive. And Pei?"

"Working as a licensed practical nurse."

"Oh, she did used to say healthcare was a potential goal of hers, so...that's great. You both are...really making something of yourselves." Her approval should make me either angry or satisfied, but somehow, I feel nothing.

"Where do you live?"

"I'm in Queens, New York."

"That's like four hours away." I'm touched she came all the way back here for my harp recital.

"Yes, it can be. If it's not too much trouble, I was hoping we could have a conversation face-to-face. You can come visit my house. There's some people here in my life I want you to meet."

"Um..." I look over at Logan, and he nods. "I think I'd like that. When are you free?"

36: Logan

We're sitting in my car in a suburb in Queens, across the street from the address Aunt Lynette gave us. We booked a hotel a week ago after we video called her and made the four-hour road trip—Wei insisted Pei stay home with the kiddo. Our trip was mostly quiet; I could tell Wei was thinking about how his reunion would go. Overall, though, I tried to get him to relax and listen to whatever radio station he wanted, a gesture he said he was grateful for.

I'm overjoyed Wei is my boyfriend again. Furthermore, he is willing to see his estranged aunt—on his terms this time, not mine.

As we sit parked in my car, the moment feels heavy as Wei stares silently out the window.

"Hey," I say, putting my hand on his knee. He turns to me. "You good?"

Wei nods then looks down at our hands on his lap. "I never told anyone this but…she reached out to us."

"What?"

He continues to gaze out the window. "Aunt

Lynette. It was the Lunar New Year a few years after she left. We still had a landline, but she called us and it went to voicemail."

I nod waiting for him to continue. "I played it once. She was just saying hi to check up on us, asking when she could visit. But I never told Pei. I was so stressed out that week. Galen was crying a lot, I had a bunch of catering shifts, neither of us were getting much sleep. I couldn't handle it all so I deleted it without telling Pei. Then I honestly forgot about it until last week."

I rub my thumb on the back of his hand. "Hey, that's completely understandable. We all have awful days. Sometimes you just shut down. I don't fault you at all."

"The next year, we cancelled our landline to save money. We both had cell phones, but she never knew our numbers. She wanted to see us again, but I stopped it." He looks up at me, his eyes glossy. "You don't think I'm awful?"

"Baby, no." I lean over and hug him. "You've had to go through so much. And she could have visited you, but she didn't. So don't blame just yourself, OK?"

Wei nods. "OK. And um, thank you...for driving me all this way and coming with me. You could have stayed at the hotel."

"No way. You needed me here, I'm here. Anything for you. We're boyfriends. That's the deal with having a romantic loser like me in your life." He chuckles, and we both exit the car.

We walk up the steps of the small brownstone house and Wei rings the doorbell.

"Whatever happens in here today..." Wei says,

staring forward and grabbing my hand. "Just know...I love you, Logan. I really love you."

I'm sorry, what?

I open my mouth, but the door opens to Aunt Lynette saying "Hey, good afternoon. Come on in, you two."

They glance at each other stoically, refraining from any physical contact, but we follow her in. I want so badly to discuss the bomb he just dropped, but this moment is for Wei's family, not me.

The house we walk through is simple, with lots of floral prints and decorations ranging from classical oil paintings to black-and-white photos. It's a warm and lived-in environment. Aunt Lynette leads us to an inner courtyard surrounded by gardens. It's a warm August day, and some butterflies float about. We sit down at a picnic table where a tray of wrapped sandwiches and some sodas await us.

"Nice place you have here," Wei says stiffly.

"Thanks. It's spacious enough for what we need. Please help yourself to some lunch." Wei and I both open up a drink. "How's the house?"

"It's still standing. Pei and I are running it as best we can. Thanks...for paying it off."

"It was the least I could do." She looks at me, then back at Wei. "So there are some things you need to know about me."

"I can go take a walk," I say. I start to get up, but Wei grabs my hand.

"No, please, I want you here." He stares into my eyes like he needs me, and I would never let him down, never again. So, I take a seat and Wei turns to his aunt. "Anything you need to say to me, you can say in front of Logan. He's... my boyfriend."

Aunt Lynette nods in understanding, then goes back to pretending I'm not there. "The thing is Wei, the reason I left you two is...Well, I'm sure you could tell, but I was never fit to be a parent."

Wei nods, staring at the table, no resentment or sadness emanating off him, only acceptance. Aunt Lynette continues. "But more importantly, I left because I needed to do some soul-searching. You see, I never felt comfortable in my own skin; not in China, and not even when we moved to New York as kids, your mother and I."

I recall Wei mentioning his aunt and his mom were sisters, and, based on old pictures, he could tell they were close. I squeeze Wei's hand, silently letting him know I'm here.

"Before I left, I started doing research online. I was looking up questions about why I feel the way I do. The truth is—" We all turn when a slender woman walks in. She's older than us, has long, gray hair with flecks of brown, and wears a salmon-colored summer dress.

"Hello there. Is this your nephew, Fa?"

"Yes. Wei, meet my romantic partner, Rainbow."

Wei looks surprised. "Nice to meet you."

"She told me you were coming. You're so handsome." She glances at me and smiles. "Hello." Turning back to Aunt Lynette, she continues. "The others are back from grocery shopping."

"Others?" Wei asks.

Aunt Lynette nods at Rainbow. "Yes, that's what I'm trying to tell you. I...no longer identify as only female. And neither does Rainbow. And neither do our other two romantic partners."

"I'm sorry?" Wei asks and my eyebrows skyrocket. *Did I hear that correctly?*

Rainbow sits next to Aunt Lynette. "I met a person named Xander online, who was polyamorous with Rainbow at the time. They taught me things about myself, things I've always suspected but never put into words. I identify as nonbinary. While some days I feel more feminine, other days I'm more masculine, and some days neither. Really, it's a spectrum for all of us. I use 'they /them' pronouns now."

Wei and I are both quiet, trying to take it all in.

"We eventually met another person named Skye and let them into our lives. Now the four of us live here. We are romantic partners, all of us. And we love each other."

Rainbow kisses Aunt Lynette on the cheek and gets up. "I'm proud of you, Fa. I'll go and help the others."

They leave and Wei still looks stunned as he nods, trying to absorb it all.

"I go by Fa now, in my personal life. Professionally, I'm still Lynette Fa Guo, a woman who works in an office here in Queens. Not everyone is understanding about my gender identity so..." She clears her throat. "Wei, I can understand... if you'd rather leave."

This snaps him out of his stupor. "Why would I want to leave? We came all the way out here."

Aunt Lynette—Fa—looks confused. "Because I just told you some rather shocking truths about me. About why I had to leave you two."

Wei grips my hand. "That's why you left? I thought you left because Pei had a baby and I realized I was gay!"

Fa shakes their head. "No. Though, truthfully, I wouldn't like the idea of sharing my space with a newborn. Child-rearing was never for me, but when my sister died...Well, you know how life was growing up for you. I wasn't as attentive as I should have been. But I would never have left simply because your sister had a baby. I went away because I couldn't face myself. Most of all, I didn't think you'd accept me. I barely accepted myself. It was...a lot for someone as lonely as me. I couldn't really take care of you kids, and I thought I was a freak for the longest time."

"You're not a freak. You're my aunt, my family!" Wei says forcefully. I'm touched to see him be so accepting, so soon. "Is it OK if we call you Aunt Lynette still? Or Aunt Fa? Or just Fa?"

Fa looks like they could burst into tears. "Aunt Fa is fine. But...you'd really accept me? I'm polyamorous, non-binary, and I was far from the ideal parent."

"Look, I know you reached out and called us that one year. I...deleted the voicemail, and eventually we got rid of the landline all together."

"Oh."

"I've regretted not calling you back." Wei reaches across the table and puts his hand on Fa's. "I want...a relationship with you. I want us to be some form of family." He puts his hand on my shoulder. "Logan taught me you shouldn't let family go, not when they're willing to reach out."

I smile, almost in tears and Wei continues. "I love you, *Ye Yi*. I know you may not have been...cut out to be a mom, but you took us in when you didn't have to. So, how about this? You live your life as happy and authentically as you want and contact us from time to time. I'm sure Galen would love to meet you. And in return, Pei and I don't want a parent, but we get to meet our Aunt Fa for the first time. Deal?"

Fa looks at him, eyes wet. "You mean all that?"

"Of course." Wei beams, looking like a weight has been lifted off his shoulders. "We can't change our childhood with you, but I'm an adult now. I want to do better for Galen. So let's start again." Fa nods, a tear rolling down their cheek. When they both get up to hug, I can't help but tear up as well.

"Thank you for forgiving me and accepting me," Fa says. They look at me over Wei's shoulder. "Both of you."

A few minutes later, Fa's three partners all come down too and the six of us have a wonderful lunch in the summer sun. Wei and I share stories all about Galen while Fa and their partners talk about their life in New York City and the home they've built together. The entire time, I exchange glances with Wei, overjoyed he's finally made peace with his estranged aunt.

I keep thinking I should feel like an outsider looking in, but I don't. When I'm with Wei, everything just fits. I remember he told me he loves me when we arrived earlier, and I want to continue that conversation so badly, but that's for later. For now, I'm letting the man I love, the one who also loves me, reconnect with his family. After today, I know this with certainty: I want to be part of Wei's family too, loving him for the rest of my life.

37: Wei

We get back to the hotel that night exhausted and emotionally drained, but in a good way. I shower first, reflecting on all I learned about Aunt Lynette—I mean, Aunt Fa—while I let the warm water wash over me. After I'm out, Logan goes in to the bathroom and I lie back on the bed in just my boxers. Once Logan showers, I call Pei and chat with her, explaining everything I've learned about our aunt and their new life.

"I'm sorry I never told you about that voicemail. It was so long ago."

"I understand why you never did," Pei says. "But...wow, that is a lot to take in."

"Yeah. But they seem so happy, so content! I invited them over in two weeks for Galen's birthday. I thought it would be a cool, low-pressure way for her to meet him. Err, *them* to meet him."

"That would be nice." She pauses over the phone. "Does she, uh, *they* seem happy?"

"Yeah, absolutely. Like a weight has been lifted

off their shoulders. Mine too. Sister, I can't wait for you to see Aunt Fa, it will be like meeting them for the first time."

"I'll take your word for it." I can hear her smile over the phone. "How do you feel though? Are you still, like...resentful?"

"Honestly, I'm starting to let that all go. Holding on to it seems so...toxic?" Logan comes out of the bathroom in just a towel and I grin. "The past is just that, in the past. Aunt Fa was going through a lot when we were kids, and what will us yelling at her accomplish? Nothing is going to give us the childhood we never got, but at least now we have our family back." Logan sits down on the bed and puts his arm around me and I cuddle into his side. "I think that's what I wanted the most, our aunt back in our lives. Don't you agree?"

"That would be great."

Logan kisses the top of my head. "Alright, I'm beat. I'm going to go sleep."

"Sure, Brother," she replies incredulously. "Tell Logan I say hi."

"Hi, Penny!" he chirps, his head next to mine. We both giggle and I bid her goodnight.

Shutting the lights, Logan pulls back the covers and hops into bed naked.

"No pajamas?" I ask, my voice teeming with innuendo.

"I didn't want anything in between us." I can almost see his grin in the darkness.

"You raise a valid point, Mr. Micucci, I should probably respect your lack of boundaries." He chuckles as I push off my boxers, then curl into his chest. My face feels his body heat and I listen to his heartbeat as he rubs my back.

"Thank you again," I mutter into his chest. "For…everything."

"It was my pleasure. But…I've been meaning to ask you something." I look up and study his face in the dark. "Before we walked into your aunt's house, you…you said something…interesting."

I'm trying to recall. "What did I say?"

"You don't remember? Oh, that's OK."

"Wait, you mean that I love you?" I ask.

"Yeah," Logan replies, his voice barely a whisper. I can tell he's looking right at me. It dawns on me maybe it's all too soon. I dragged his ass into my family drama four hours away. It's possible I'm asking too much of him.

"Oh, it's OK, you can forget it. We can pretend it never happened."

"But I don't want to forget!" he exclaims.

"What?"

"I don't want to pretend it never happened. Wei, I didn't get to reply before, but I've been thinking about it all day. No one's ever said they loved me before." I pull up and look right into his eyes, hungry as they are in the dark. "Wei, I love you too."

Those familiar fireworks go off in my heart again. "Really?"

"Yes. God, so much. I've wanted you since before you kissed me under the mistletoe. Watching your music lecture every week was like torture because I think I was slowly falling for you the entire time!"

"No way." I chuckle.

"Yes! Now you're not my professor anymore. You're my co-faculty, my neighbor, my boyfriend…and the love of my life. Being with you feels like discovering my favorite song on repeat."

"But won't that get played out?" I ask.

"So far, no. With you, it's like music is brand new, and I never want to be without you. I'm sorry if this is all coming on too strong, but you need to know I'm in this, Wei. You're it for me. I love you, and—"

I cut off his declaration of love with a kiss. In a day filled with emotional breakthroughs, this takes the cake. I need Logan to know I feel the same way, that he's all I'll ever need. I want us to play music for the rest of our lives together, even when we're old and gray and grown-up Galen has to take care of us. Logan makes everything in my life better and I don't see myself ever letting him go.

I kiss his neck, and he moans. I pull back the cover and kiss his fantastic chest—all muscular with tufts of hair—and he pushes upward when I catch each nipple. I feel him get hard, and I bring my mouth lower, tasting his abs.

"Wei...what are you—"

"Let me please you? I love you, Logan, and I want to please you."

"OK," he huffs, his hips squirming underneath my breath. Soon enough, I'm stroking his cock, bringing it to a steely hardness.

"Ooh," he moans underneath me. I lick the tip, and he squirms even more. I put my mouth over the swollen head and he cries out, not caring about the other guests in the hotel.

I lick, pump, and swallow him down, giving him all the ecstasy I can because I want him to feel at least half as good as he makes me feel. Sex is fun, but any two bodies can do that; real emotional connection and love, though? It's priceless.

"Wei, fuck, I love you…I'm—" That's all he gets out before he grunts and unloads into my mouth. I take it all in, hoping he knows I want to be with him, our bodies intertwined, for the rest of my life.

38: Logan

Wei reaches up and puts the red-and-blue paper cone hat on my head. The string strap hurts my chin a bit, but his smile makes it all worth it. "There, now it's a party," he says, putting on his own party hat.

"You're going to make me puke." I turn to see Omar sticking his tongue out, and Kareem, Ravi, and Paul are standing next to him shaking their heads, looking unimpressed. "You two are adorable and gross."

"This is a private event!" I declare with faux-anger. "No student-athlete-knuckleheads allowed."

"Hey, Wei invited us!" Ravi says, putting his hands up in defeat.

I turn to my boyfriend who's smiling and shrugging. "Can't have a soccer-themed birthday party without soccer players right? Well, sports-themed, anyway."

Today, we have plenty of party decorations set up inside the Athletics Center events space. There's a long table with colorful table cloth, balloons, napkins, plates, and drinks. Pei is talking to some other mothers from Galen's class, and four kids are playing catch with foam footballs I provided.

It has been two weeks since our family trip to Queens. The semester doesn't start for another two days, so I insisted we hold Galen's eighth birthday right here in my baby, the Athletics Center. Wei and I have been coordinating, inviting, and gathering supplies for the best party a soon-to-be-third grader could ask for.

"I guess we could use a few clowns," I remark.

"Please, you love us," Omar says and the other boys chuckle.

"Speaking of clowns, where's Landon?"

Ravi, Paul, and Omar grimace. "He's...not in a good mood," Kareem replies. Ah, I know what that means: young heartbreak. Wei hands out some hats and Omar, Paul, and Kareem put theirs on.

"Is your boyfriend coming?" Wei asks.

"Yeah, but he's getting his brother, the one who just started at KU. I hope you don't mind, since Landon's not coming."

"Not at all. We've got plenty of food!" Wei chirps.

"Steven's brother is coming?" Omar asks.

"Yeah, he's cool. Hey, let's go grab some foam footballs!" Ravi says, tapping Kareem and Paul on the shoulders. The three walk to where the kids are, but Omar stays behind.

He frowns and yanks off the paper cone hat. "You alright?" I ask.

"I'm fine. Is my hair all messed up?"

Wei and I shrug. "I'll use the bathroom then, real quick." He disappears, but before I can ask, another guest arrives.

"Hey guys."

"Felipe? What are you doing here?" Wei asks.

"For the uh...birthday boy?" He waves a small blue envelope.

"I invited him!" Pei says behind us. We both turn to see her rushing up to us. "Hi, Felipe. Nice to see you."

"Hey, Penny," he replies, his glasses starting to fog up for some reason. She touches his elbow and they walk back to where all the parents are.

Wei stares at them perplexed. "Um..." He turns back to me. "Did you...did you know?"

I raise my hands. "No clue! The guy taught me 'Habañera' but we did *not* talk about our personal lives."

Wei opens his mouth to ask more, but we both hear a familiar high-pitched voice.

"Logie!" Aggie is walking up to us holding a tray of cupcakes, and Otis is behind her, holding a green gift bag. "And Wei-Ee! My two favorite lovebirds!" She gives us both a cheek kiss and beams. "I'm so *thrilled* to be able to hang out with you all when I'm not wearing a sweatband."

"Thanks for coming, Aggie," I say. I really am glad to be able to call her a friend now that she's not constantly throwing herself at me. Much. "Otis, were you two...?"

"I was uh, lost!" he replies, his deep voice echoing through the large events space. "And Mrs. Hark found me, realized we're going the same way, and well...here we are!"

"It's *Miss* Hark," she says, with a dramatic eye-roll. "I'm certainly not married."

"Of course, my mistake," Otis says. I look

between the two of them, trying to process this conversation.

"Could you be a dear and open up a chair for me, Otis?" Aggie asks.

"Certainly!" They leave us and walk to the large table where Felipe and Pei are deep in conversation.

Eyebrows raised, I glance at Wei, who looks at me, visibly confused. We both break out in laughter at the same time and I hold him by his hips. "This party is turning out to be...enlightening."

"I know," Wei says. "We definitely got Galen a party for the books, and I doubt he even notices all the adults flirting around him."

Pei walks back to where we're standing and looks behind us. We turn around and spot Aunt Fa, holding a large red gift bag. They look timid, like they're doing something wrong, but the smile on Wei's face tells me everything is going to be OK.

"Hi, Logan...Wei...uh, Pei." Pei nods and, after hesitating, she moves in to hug her aunt. They hold each other for a long ten seconds, and Galen strides right up to us.

"Hey, kiddo, we'd like you to meet someone," Wei says, crouching down to his nephew. "Remember what we told you?"

He nods his little head, and Pei pulls away, leaving Aunt Fa face-to-face with Galen.

"Hello," they say and nod stiffly.

"Hi!" Galen waves.

"I'm your Aunt Fa. I heard you are the birthday boy." They hand him the gift bag.

Galen grins and takes it then looks inside. He pulls out a massive soccer ball with the cardboard still around it, fresh from the store.

"Wow!" Galen says.

"What do you say to your Aunt Fa?" Pei prompts him.

"Your pronouns are 'they/them'!" he recites, like he's been studying it all day. We all chuckle, but Aunt Fa looks like they could just about shatter in happiness.

"What else?" Pei asks.

"Thank you!" Galen wraps his arms around Aunt Fa and I notice a tear rolling down their face.

"You're quite welcome."

Wei pats Galen on the shoulder. "Hey, why don't you go ask Kareem to help you open the ball?"

Galen nods and runs off, back to where all the boys, both little and college-aged, are playing with foam footballs.

"Thank you...for coming," Wei says.

"Thank you for inviting me." Fa wipes their eyes.

"Come on," Pei taps their shoulder. "I'll introduce you to some people I know." The two of them walk over to Felipe and the other moms.

Later on, once Steven and his brother arrive, we all gather to have some pizza and hot dogs, which Wei had delivered courtesy of his catering friends. Galen wants to keep playing, but Kareem convinces him eating food is an essential part of every athlete's daily life.

Afterwards, we bring out the cake and sing for Galen. Otis is kind enough to take many pictures of Pei, Wei, and Fa, all gathered around the kiddo. At one point, Otis insists I join in on the pictures, and Wei beckons me, so I oblige. Looking around at the table, feeling Wei by my side holding me, it all seems so perfect. I gaze at Aggie, Otis, and even the soccer boys, and everything slots into place. These people are my loved ones, and this can be my family now.

We all applaud after Galen blows out the candles on the soccer-ball-shaped cake and I start to tear up. Everything about this moment is perfect, and it's all thanks to this gorgeous man on my arm walking by my office door all those months ago.

"What's wrong?" Wei asks, once everyone is lining up for cake slices.

"Nothing," I reply, wiping my eye. "For once, nothing is wrong." I lean in and kiss him, hoping he knows all the ways I cherish him.

39: Wei

I finish up my set in the Athletics Center and the students that were slow dancing all applaud, then walk back to their seats. In the crowd, Paul, my former student, is one of the only athletes I recognize. It's been exactly two years since that fateful night I met Logan. Ravi, Steven, and their whole batch have graduated and moved on. There's a magical nostalgia whenever I see the Christmas lights throughout the events space, reminding me of the romance I felt that evening. I look at the tables of this year's Athletics Formal, and my boyfriend's seat is empty. Huh.

Professor Reyes takes me by the arm. "You deserve a break, Professor Wong."

"Yes, but I'm here to perform, not eat." My instinct to listen to her every word is strong. I'm no longer her Assistant Professor, but a full-fledged professor in my own right; Felipe and I are almost done completing our doctorates in the twenty-three months we've been working at KU. Reyes is still the head of the music department, so I still occasionally have to do what she says.

"No, no, go sit down where your other half was

sitting." She leads me forward and Paul beams at me, opening up Logan's chair. Next to it, Coach Dacks is grinning, giving me a thumbs-up. That man has never even acknowledged my existence. *Why is everyone acting so weird?*

The audience eating dinner comes to a hush when I spot Logan walking up to the piano on stage. *What's he doing up there?* I turn to Paul and see him taking out his phone and smiling at me. To my left, Coach Dacks gives me yet another thumbs-up and points at Logan. Everyone around me is taking out their phones or smiling directly at me.

Huh?

Soon enough, Logan starts playing the unmistakable first few measures of 'If I Ain't Got You' by the iconic Alicia Keys. He's doing so well, and I am floored; I knew he practiced here and there at the house—I moved into his giant mansion over the summer—but this is something else! He never told me he was going to be performing at the Athletics Formal. Why would he keep this a secret from me?

He gets through the entire song and I'm moved. There's an uproar of applause, Coach Dacks is whistling with his fingers, but I'm too in shock to move. Logan is... incredible. He takes my breath away constantly, even after all this time. We go on dates, sleep together every night, spend a lot of time looking after Galen, and being with Logan never gets old. He loves listening to me play the harp, and now it seems he's really taken piano playing seriously.

I didn't think I could fall in love with this man any more, yet here we are; Logan Micucci never ceases to enchant me.

I'm so moved I barely have time to register him taking the microphone and walking up to me.

"I have some things to say. And, since I'm the Facilities Manager here, you all have to listen." There are smatterings of laughter, but I'm still confused. Logan's not one to draw attention to himself for no reason.

"Wei Wong." He walks forward, and now all eyes are on me. I tense up in the chair, still not sure what's happening. "I've made it no secret how crazy I am about you. I love living with you, I love listening to you play music, I love being a part of your family, but most of all, I love getting to be your boyfriend. Overall, that makes me a selfish prick, because I want you all to myself."

There are some "*aww's*" and laughter, and my throat goes dry. *Is he doing what I think he's doing?* "The song I just played should tell you everything you need to know. Everything in the world doesn't matter if I don't have you by my side."

He gets down on one knee and I swear time stops. No one else is in the building, and there's a buzzing in my ears. *Yes, he's doing exactly what I've dreamed of for so long.*

"Wei, I want to love you until my dying day. You make the strings in my heart play a symphony." He takes out a small black box from his coat pocket. "Please do me the honor of being my husband." When he opens the box, I see the glimmer of a small diamond ring. "Wei, will you marry me?"

I finally take in a breath and nod, unable to speak. My eyes are watery as I fling myself at him, getting on my knees to hug him. I pull back and kiss him, tears staining both of our faces. There's some applause as I pull back and he puts the ring on my finger—at least, I think there is. When Logan kisses me, all I hear is a symphony, too.

Epilogue: Logan

I stand in one of the back rooms of the banquet hall, staring at myself in the mirror. I must say: I look good in my tux and my pink tulip boutonnière. I keep readjusting my neck tie for no reason other than to keep my hands busy.

"Would you stop fidgeting?" Otis says, sitting in the chair next to me. "You're not getting cold feet now, are you?"

I smile. "No, absolutely not." Wei and I jumped into the wedding planning headfirst and managed to book this late summer wedding. We've only been engaged for eight months or so, but hey—when you know, you know. "It's just...all those eyes on me."

"I was like that, too, at my wedding. But when I saw my wife, God rest her soul, walking down the aisle, marriage felt like the most natural thing in the world." I smile, thinking about Wei walking down the aisle. I haven't seen him all day, so I'm itching to get my hands on him. I don't do well being apart from him for too long.

Dating Wei these past two-plus years or so has

been nothing short of a dream. Sure, we have our differences and our arguments, but nothing quite as bad as when I went behind his back—never doing that again. Still, we never stay mad for too long, and hold each other every night.

He's made my life better, not only by giving me the family I've always needed, but by supporting me. At his suggestion, I've attended a few therapy sessions to help cope with the trauma I'm still holding on to. I'm certainly less triggered now by car accidents in the snow, and my smiles at work are more genuine. He's held my hand whenever I've visited my parents' graves, and I've done the same for him, even though he has less baggage about his family. Speaking of, Aunt Fa has been visiting from time to time, and we all get along well.

I once thought my life was over, but now I have a family to look forward to growing old with. Wei continues to make my life a joyous symphony, as corny as that sounds.

"This is the most natural thing for me too, Otis." I turn to him and he gets up. "Thank you. For everything."

He puts his hand on my shoulder, and his eyes start to get wet. "Your father and mother would absolutely be so proud of the man you've become. And when you walk down that aisle, just know their love is with you."

I wipe away a tear, but when I open my mouth, I hear Aggie's familiar shrill voice at the doorway. "Game time, boys. This is *not* a drill!"

Otis and I smirk and roll our eyes. "I better get to the front before my girlfriend, the wedding planner, yanks me out of here by the ear." I nod and he claps my shoulder one last time. Otis and Aggie dating was bizarre at first, but now seeing how happy they make each other only makes me smile.

After a moment of solitude, I feel a presence behind me.

"You look great."

I turn to Pei. "Thanks. You do, too."

"But it's *your* wedding. And my brother's."

"How's he doing? And where's the little man?"

"He's fine, all dolled up and ready to walk down the aisle, like you." She moves in and adjusts my tie. "And Galen insisted on sitting next to Kareem, Omar, and the others."

"Of course," I reply. After she's done, we look at each other, a silent moment passing between us. "Thank you. For accepting me since day one."

"Since the day you walked out of my brother's room into our kitchen?" We both laugh. "I didn't have much of a choice. Wei finally found a man, I wasn't gonna stop him."

"But still, thank you. For letting me into your family." A tear rolls down her face, and we lean in and hug, hard.

"Thank you for giving Wei all the things I know he deserves." I nod and finally let go. "Come on. Let's get you married to my brother." She takes my arm, and we walk out the door.

I think I'm done crying when Pei and I walk down the aisle first. Felipe, now Pei's boyfriend, and Professor Reyes play the traditional 'Canon in D' by Pachelbel on the cello and violin, respectively. The banquet hall looks absolutely stunning, and everything about this moment is picture-perfect. I manage to keep my eyes dry when I get to the altar where Otis, our lawful officiant, waits in his tux.

I think I'm good until everyone stands up, seeing two silhouettes at the doorway; Aunt Fa, in their navy blue suit, holding Wei, in his white tuxedo. The moment he starts walking down the aisle and makes eye-contact with me, I'm a goner. The tears just keep. Coming. Out. And sobs too. It's embarrassing.

He's so perfect. And he completes my life in every way. *Fuck*, I'm the luckiest man in the world.

The ceremony begins and I can't even concentrate. All I can do is stare at Wei. Galen walks up with the two rings and we take turns putting them on each other while Otis says things I can't listen to; I'm too busy wiping away my tears.

"And now, the vows," Otis says, breaking me out of my spell.

Wei takes out a piece of paper and holds my hand. "Logan, when I took that teaching job at Korham University, I thought all the puzzle pieces in my life were finally falling into place. I didn't realize it was because I was about to meet the most amazing, supportive, handsome guy in the universe. Being with you has been the greatest joy of my life. When you're around, I don't need anything else. I'm less alone, less broken, and less incomplete. *You're* my home Logan, and I want to spend the rest of my life being your husband. It's just like you said the night you confessed your feelings to me years ago; you're harmony to me."

Aw shit.

I try really hard to wipe my tears quickly and maintain my composure, but I can't stop sobbing. Otis hands me a handkerchief and I dab my eyes and give it back to him. People are probably laughing, but I don't care. I take out the paper with my vows and clear my throat.

"Let me try to get through this without sobbing." Wei chuckles, and I smile. "Wei, before I met you, I was a hollow shell of a man. You were the only one who made me feel a spark of happiness after years of feeling dull and gray. You taught me how to play music, but you were really teaching me how to live again."

Wei starts to tear up, and I clear my throat and continue. "Thank you for granting me the honor of being part of your life, of your family. You've given me so much more than money and possessions could ever be worth. Thank you for giving me something to look forward to: being your husband, and now, after today, growing old with you." I crumple up the paper and shove it in my pocket. "You're harmony to me, too."

I reach up and wipe Wei's eyes and he tries to stifle something between a sob and a laugh. Otis clears his throat. "Do you, Wei Wong, take this man to be your husband?"

"I do."

"And do you, Logan Micucci, take this man to be your husband?"

"Heck yeah, I do." We all chuckle, and I squeeze Wei's hands a little more.

Otis smiles at both of us. "Then by the power invested in me by the state of New York, I now pronounce you husband and husband. Now kiss already!"

Wei takes my face in his hands and we do just that—kiss, in front of all of our loved ones applauding.

Forever is a long time, but it won't be silent with Wei Wong as my husband. We're only going to hear music.

(The End)

213

Thank You

Dear Reader,

Thanks for going on this romance journey with me! I'm ecstatic to be able to share Wei and Logan's story with the world. I know I say this every time, but this was a labor of love. I hope the emotional roller-coaster was as thrilling for you to read as much as it was for me to write. That final chapter pulls my heart strings every time! I got married around the time of this book's release and I'm very much a beginner at the harp, so needless to say, Wei and Logan's story holds a special place in my heart.

See below for my other works and go to the next page for all my socials. I'm obsessed with chatting with folks who've enjoyed my books. Don't be shy about private messaging me! An honest but respectful review would be SO so helpful, so please consider leaving one on Amazon.

The next book is the final novel in the A&A series. I think there's one last couple of guys whom you all met in book one who need a spotlight on their love story, don't you think so?

* * *

Never stop loving life and never stop reading,
  CD Rachels

Acknowledgments

Huge thank you to Saskia for volunteering to do a sensitivity check about nonbinary topics. Thanks to Rod—the best book friend I could have asked for. Thanks to Rachel, my original fan. Thanks Molly for letting me ramble at odd hours. Thanks to the established M/M online authors who give me advice and let me pop into their groups to advertise. For Catherine and Karen and the team at StoryStyling Cover Designs and GRR: you all took this book from being a dream to being a reality. And last, but never least, every Chill Discoursian who has ever messaged me or left a review—it means more to me than I could ever express.

Other Works by CD

1. What happened when Ravi, the soccer star, was forced to take an art class? Check out "The Lines We Draw" Artists and Athletes book 1.

2. What happened when Landon wanted to turn over a new leaf all while taking a dance class? Check out "The Moves We Make" Artists and Athletes book 2.

3. What happens when Dominic goes to grad school and meets his online video game buddy? For the FREE novella on Kindle delivered via Prolific Works check out "The Games We Love" Artists and Athletes book 2.5.

3. Want to be front row for the final curtain call for our Korham University soccer boys? Look out for "The Roles We Own" Artists and Athletes book 4.

About the Author

About the Author

CD Rachels has been coming up with stories since he was little. At first it was all about superheroes and pocket monsters, but his genre of choice has expanded since puberty.

He's been consuming young adult gay fiction since he was a teen, but within the past five years, he's moved up to the big leagues of gay adult romance. In 2020 during quarantine, he burned through more male/male romance books than he ever had in the previous 29 years combined.

He lives in New York City with the love of his life and works in health insurance. When he's not reading and writing, he's playing board games and practicing music. He is honored to become a published author, and if you're reading this, your support means so much to him that he has goosebumps just thinking about it.

Be the first to hear about all his updates and new releases!

Sign up for his newsletter "The Chill Discourse Report"

Follow him on Instagram: @cdrachels

Join his Facebook group where he hosts polls and chats with readers nonstop: "CD Rachels' Chill Discourse Room"

Follow/review his other works on Goodreads here

Check him out on BookBub too here

72362619R00126